DEAD WOLF WALKING
SHAPES OF AUTUMN: BOOK THREE

VERONICA BLADE

Gardnerville, Nevada

DEAD WOLF WALKING

Crush Publishing, Inc
1291 Bolivia Way,
Gardnerville, NV 89460
www.CrushPublishing.com

Crush Publishing, Inc name and logo are trademarks of Crush
Publishing, Inc and are used only with its permission.

The places, characters and events portrayed in this book are ficti-
tious. Any similarity to real persons, living or dead, is coinciden-
tal and not intended by author.

ISBN 978-0-9910756-5-2

Cover design and layout by Rose Nomura

Printed in the United States of America

DEAD WOLF WALKING
SHAPES OF AUTUMN, BOOK THREE

EXCERPT

AS WE DREW nearer to the mansion, not a soul was in sight. If anyone was around, they certainly kept well hidden.

"There's something... something different about this place." Zack studied the row of hedges that merged with a clump of trees, then stared at the building a long moment. "Just don't know what."

Well good. I preferred Zack on alert. Maybe this meant he was back, some part of him at least. I had Cedric Gallagher and his "different" environment to thank for it.

As soon as I opened the driver's side door, I felt it. A strange energy not unlike my own, but definitely not shape-shifter or werewolf. What the hell were these people?

Zack arrived at my side and laced his fingers through mine as someone dropped from the roof—which was four stories up—and landed in front of us with a thud. My ribs tensed and we took an instinctive step back.

The man's lip curled up, exposing long white fangs. "Werewolves."

I didn't correct him on the plural part. Better if he had no clue I was a shape-shifter who was consorting with a werewolf. My mother may have had faith in

Cedric, but that didn't mean we were safe from every-one else he associated with. Any one of them could turn us in for a reward. "We're here to see Cedric Gallagher," I said.

His dark blond hair skittered over his forehead when he folded his arms over his muscular chest. "For what purpose?"

I inhaled again, caught the sweet metallic scent, and it hit me. What other life form could smell so strongly of blood? *Vampires*, I told Zack silently. From what little I'd read in the books Zack's father had left for him, vampires hated werewolves.

In daylight? This is not good, he said.

Yeah, like I didn't already realize that.

FOR ZANE RAE BLADE

I love you more than mocha.

CHAPTER ONE
—— *Autumn* ——

WITH OUR LEGS tangled together in the sheets, Zack pressed so close to me, a gnat couldn't slip between us. His hips lay flush against mine, his nearly two hundred pounds of solid muscle weighing me down against the mattress like a heavenly anchor.

His hand swept slowly along my side, inching my tank top up, his hot mouth trailing kisses over my shoulder and setting my skin ablaze. My head angled to the side and my lungs quivered on a soft, lusty sigh as his lips burned a path over my shoulder and up my neck.

As much as I would've loved to drag Zack to my empty house two blocks away and be alone with him, we both knew where that could lead. Werewolves didn't associate in any way with shape-shifters. As if being able to morph into a multitude of forms instead of just one made us inferior. Not only was it against werewolf law for Zack to treat me as an equal in any way, but mixing species—having sex—was believed to make both sides weaker.

I suspected that to be a myth though. But what if I was wrong? Neither of us could afford to lose our powers if we were going to be on the run soon and fighting for our lives. No matter how much we both wanted to abandon all logic and reason, we refused to allow our hormones to take over.

But we could reap every last ounce of pleasure from the things we could still do.

Reduced to ragged breaths, I arched up, my mouth capturing his. He groaned into my mouth and I drank him in, not sure how much more I could take without ripping his clothes off. I stifled the urge to moan. Sure, everyone in his house—his mom, his aunt Cara and uncle Mac, his cousin Trevor, and probably Trevor's younger brothers—knew I snuck into Zack's room most nights. We weren't usually doing much more than sleeping, but since they all assumed more, the whole situation was embarrassing enough. So I opted to pretend everyone was oblivious to my presence.

Zack's arms straightened and he lifted off me, his arms flexing as they took the bulk of his weight. He cocked his head.

"Everything okay?" I asked, running my fingers through his dark tousled hair.

He rolled off me, his feet landing on the floor. "What's that noise?"

With my shape-shifter perceptions, I could hear as well as Zack or any other werewolf. I tensed, alert for the slightest sound. There it was again, coughing from somewhere in the house. Or choking. Zack rocketed off the bed, snatched a T-shirt off the chair, and threw it on as he sprinted out of the room so fast I forgot to pretend not to be there.

I heard the sound again, like someone gasping for air, and leaped off Zack's bed to navigate the near-black hallway on my way to his mom's room. In the dim lighting from the bedside lamp, Zack leaned over Favianne, her long, dark brown hair partially obscuring her too-pale olive skin.

"Mom, wake up!" Zack held her by the shoulders. "Mom! Mom! Wake up," he demanded, his voice breaking.

Struggling for oxygen hadn't woken her and she wasn't responding to Zack's jostling. That had to be bad. My heart pounded as I skirted to the other side of the bed to lay my ear against Favianne's chest. Her pulse seemed agonizingly slow and her lungs sounded like sandpaper scraping.

"We need to get her to a hospital," I said, ready to dart back into Zack's room for my cell.

He grabbed her phone on the nightstand and dialed 9-1-1. Moments later, he'd given the operator all the info and hit the end button. "I've never seen her this way," he said. "A couple of months ago when we took her to the hospital for pneumonia, she was at least conscious."

I didn't want to think about what her lack of response might mean. I chewed my lip, my throat swelling. If we lost Favianne because Zack and I hadn't acted fast enough, I'd never forgive myself. "Wouldn't it be quicker to load her up and drive her there ourselves?"

"Your car is at your house and I'm afraid my Jeep will be too bumpy." Zack gathered her frail body into his arms, and I skirted around him. He was already tall, practically towering over my five-eight. He dwarfed his mother even more. She had lost so much weight since we graduated high school only a few weeks ago. I couldn't imagine her having it in her to go another day. Tears wet my lashes as I held the front door open for Zack.

His aunt Cara burst into the living room, cinching her bathrobe closed. It didn't take a genius to figure out where we were taking her sister. "It's bad, isn't it?" she asked, using the back of her hand to brush away dark wisps of hair from her forehead.

"I don't know." But I did know, and my pulse hammered at my temple.

In the distance, red and white lights flashed against the night sky as an ambulance turned the corner and came into view. I jogged to the curb and stood beside Zack an instant before the ambulance pulled to a stop. Two paramedics gingerly transferred Favianne to a gurney. With his arms free of his mother, Zack slumped, a deep line etched between his brows.

The EMTs secured Favianne inside the ambulance, then closed the doors. The garage opened behind us as Cara bustled down the porch stairs and jingled her keys. Zack's shoes dangled from two fingers of her other hand. "We can follow them in my car. Jump in."

I touched his hand, my teeth digging into my bottom lip to keep it from trembling. "I need to stop at my house. I'll get the Mustang and see you there as soon as I can."

Zack dropped a peck on my cheek, then rushed up the driveway and into Cara's car. I waved to him before doubling back inside to his room. Halfway down the hallway, I froze. This was it. I knew it in my gut. For weeks I'd been dreading this moment when Favianne would leave us. Zack had been expecting it for years. No one had thought she would live this long, but she'd surpassed everyone's expectations.

At least I'd had several months to fall in love with her sweet smiles, subtle humor, and fierce love for Zack. That was about to end. Deep down, Zack knew it too. And he wouldn't want to waste one minute of his last moments with her. No way would he leave the hospital anytime soon.

Hustling into his closet, I jumped high enough for my hands to touch the top shelf and reach his duffel bag. My gaze caught on the black box his mom had given him a couple of months ago and insisted he take. It contained documents, bank records, a passport, and everything he needed to access the money his father had left him.

If Favianne did indeed die, Zack would have to get as far away from Los Angeles as possible or else Renzo Soriano would very likely try to escort him to the werewolf king where he'd serve the crown or be assigned to a pack—which Zack had already declared to me he would never do.

Unless Renzo felt no loyalty to the werewolf king. In that case, we had nothing to worry about. But I couldn't be sure either way. Renzo had mysteriously shown up at the coffee shop weeks ago and he'd never said much about anything other than he was "on vacation." Yet he always seemed to be around, and I couldn't figure out what he wanted.

We couldn't take the chance that he was setting us up. Zack's only choice was to run and his best chance of escaping Renzo—and every other werewolf scout—would be to leave from the hospital without returning home.

From the moment Zack and I had gotten together, we'd known our relationship was doomed. Traveling together and breaking werewolf law by associating in any way other than master and slave would attract attention and paint a big, fat target on our backs. We'd already agreed that when Zack left, I'd stay. We vowed to enjoy each other for however long we had and not talk about the end.

But Renzo knew I was a shape-shifter and he barely tolerated me as it was. He'd been hostile toward me from the beginning and I never knew why, other than the obvious—he was a werewolf naturally predisposed to not liking my kind. What if, once Zack left, Renzo couldn't find a reason to let me live? No way could I stay behind, alone. I'd have to gather my things and be ready to meet up with my shape-shifter parents.

For the past few weeks, Zack had been sneaking clothes to me in preparation for his imminent escape and I'd been hiding them in my room. But if Zack was leaving for good, he'd need more. I loaded the black box into the duffel bag and then located some of his favorite jeans and T-shirts, boxers, socks, his laptop, a razor, his toothbrush, and black boots.

After zipping up the bag, I swung it over my shoulder and padded into the dim hallway.

"Hey." Zack's uncle, Mac, threaded his fingers through his thinning red hair. "What's with the big bag?"

I forced my hands still, battling the adrenaline racing through my veins. Mac didn't need to know I was slightly panicked over my and Zack's inevitable need to flee. "Zack won't want to leave Favianne's side. He'll need a change of clothes, his phone, laptop. Stuff like that."

He nodded, his expression grave. "I'll be taking off for the hospital as soon as the boys are ready. If there's any news before I get there, would you ask Cara to call me?"

"Sure. But I need to stop at home first. You'll probably beat me there." I offered a small smile before heading out the door.

Despite the weight of Zack's duffel bag, I made good time down the two blocks to my house. Thankfully, I'd backed the Mustang into the driveway earlier and pulled it alongside the neighbor's fence. Much easier to get something through the window and into the trunk without being spotted. I squeezed by the side of the house to the rear of my car, which was obscured by bushes, and tossed his bag in the trunk of my car, then hurried inside to shower.

Knowing I'd be at a hospital for a while, then possibly traveling to who knew where, I gathered my now-shoulder-length hair into a low ponytail. Good thing I'd cut off my long tresses a few weeks ago. I'd had a feeling I'd need a simple hairstyle the next few months. Or years.

As I sped through my house a few short minutes later spotting things I needed, an ache mounted in my chest. An ache I didn't think would go away anytime soon.

Even if I got to the hospital in time, my gut told me we were losing her. She probably wasn't going to wake up and it was too late to say good-bye. And I wasn't at the hospital to comfort Zack. But the chance was too great that he and I couldn't return to our houses. We'd very likely be leaving our home, our friends, for parts unknown. I had to be ready, because I had no idea how many werewolves were out there and how many of them the king would have hunting Zack.

CHAPTER TWO
—— *Zack* ——

I JOGGED AFTER the paramedics pushing the gurney through the emergency entrance of the hospital. They wheeled my mom toward another set of double doors and as they swung open in welcome, a woman in scrubs strode toward me, a stethoscope hanging from her neck. I attempted to follow my mother, but the woman stood in my path and blocked my way. I started forward to go around her, and she thrust out an arm, stopping me. "Personnel only beyond this point," she said.

Antiseptic and chemicals stung my nose as I peered over her shoulder, watching the gurney disappear around the corner. "I'm family."

"I'm sorry. Personnel only." She shook her head.

"She's going to be okay, right?" I coached myself not to shove the woman aside and tear through the corridor. But if my mom had a chance of being saved, I needed to allow the doctors to do their job. I backed off, putting more distance between my mother and myself.

"We'll do everything we can," she tossed over her

shoulder and then vanished behind the double doors.

A soft hand stroked my back and I turned around to see Winnie, her chin quivering. The warm smile that usually greeted us was absent from her face. "Oh, honey, I just heard about your mother. I'm so sorry."

"Thanks, Winnie." I stooped and folded her into a hug, barely getting my arms around her thick middle. My mom loved Winnie and by now the hospital staff knew to always assign her to my mom anytime she had an appointment. I hoped today would be no different. "Always good to see you."

"You're such a good boy." Her mouth trembled before she gave my hand a quick squeeze. "I'll go check on her and be back as soon as I can." She swished away in her colorful scrubs, and I prayed this visit wouldn't be the last time Winnie attended to my mom.

Alone again, I paced the waiting room, unable to stand still. My mom couldn't die. We'd had scares before due to her autoimmune disorder, but she'd always come through. She was a survivor and she'd get past this too. She had to. But what if she didn't?

CHAPTER THREE
——— *Autumn* ———

SINCE I DIDN'T know how long I'd be gone, I probably needed more than the emergency bag I kept in my car. I could morph into a ferocious bear and kill a werewolf, but I was still a girl. I wanted my stuff with me.

After I'd overfilled a large suitcase, I stood at the front door of my empty house. I gazed forlornly at the tidy modern kitchen, then let my eyes follow the length of the house—the perfectly distressed wood floors, the sparse furniture, the soft pastel walls and white trim—my gaze ending at the staircase. I'd probably never again climb the steps to my room and lie on my purple comforter. My naked toes may never again glide through the white faux fur rug at the foot of my bed.

On a long, deep inhale, I said a silent good-bye to the only real home I'd known. I dragged my luggage to the dining room and crammed it through the side window so that it dropped onto the driveway. I slithered through after my stuff, then opened the trunk as quietly as I could.

After backtracking through the window, I locked up the house, exited out the front door, then headed to the hospital. I fervently hoped Favianne hadn't already passed, that she'd wake up and Zack would get the chance to talk to her.

By the time I got to the hospital and parked, over an hour had flown by. Tiny wisps of light on the horizon hinted that daylight would soon come. Cara met me in the emergency waiting room, her lips a grim line as she hugged me. "It doesn't look good. Zack's going to need you to be strong."

Tears pooled in my eyes and I sniffed as she released me. "That's not going to be easy. What did the doctors say?"

"Her organs are shutting down, one by one." She let out a shuddering breath. "My sister has a do-not-resuscitate order. If her heart stops or her kidneys shut down, they can't do CPR or hook her up to a machine."

Oh, God. Poor Cara, about to lose her only sister. I clutched her hand. "Did she ever wake up?"

"No," she whispered, her gaze lowering to the short, tan carpet.

My body went slack and my tongue refused to budge. The automatic doors to the emergency rooms swung open and Zack emerged, his skin pallid. Was his mom gone? Abandoning Cara, I sped into Zack's arms and buried my face in his neck.

"So glad you're finally here," he said, holding me

tightly.

We stayed that way for what seemed like minutes, my arms wrapped around his waist and my cheek resting against his shoulder. He loosened his hold and I studied his red, swollen eyes, wishing I could take away his grief.

"The doctor told us to say our good-byes, but how am I supposed to do that if she doesn't wake up?" he asked, his voice hoarse.

"You have to believe she knows you're here, Zack." What else could I say? I attempted to do the impossible and comfort him. "She knows you love her."

Zack pressed his forehead to mine, his lids drooping. "Don't go anywhere, okay?"

I cupped his cheeks. "I'm staying right here."

Zack watched Cara speaking to a man in a white lab coat. I listened in.

"She doesn't have long, a few hours at the most." The man in the lab coat waited a beat and his voice softened. "I'm sorry, but with a DNR order, we're limited in what we can do. Mrs. De Luca made it clear she didn't want to be kept alive artificially. Her heart's going to give up soon and when it does…"

Zack inhaled sharply. This really *was* it. That wonderful, sweet woman would never again call me *Tesora* or gently scold Zack for being so stubborn, and she'd never again lecture me on sticking by him.

Zack brushed his thumb across my skin to dry my cheek as if trying to erase my sadness. "I need to spend these last moments with her."

My heart was imploding on itself, but I somehow convinced my lips to form words. "Of course you do. I'll check on Cara." If people were going to stand vigil until the end, it should be her family.

"She loves you too, Autumn. You should be in there with us."

"Give me a couple of minutes, okay?" Hopefully that would be enough time to compose myself.

He slogged toward the door to the rooms and disappeared. Cara's shoulders hunched as she stared at a wall and hugged her elbows. She looked like I felt. But if she kept that up in the waiting room and didn't say good-bye to her sister, she'd probably regret it the rest of her life.

"C'mon." I curled my hand around hers.

"I'm not sure I can." Cara's eyes glistened and her voice broke. "I can't stand by and watch my sister die."

Even Cara knew it was the end. Icy fingers chilled my spine. "She's not dead forever, just going somewhere else, a place where she's healthy and no longer in pain." I gave Cara's hand a gentle tug and she let me lead her through the door.

"This one." She motioned toward a room ahead.

Favianne's scent wafted into the hallway and I slowed to let Cara pass me. Favianne always smelled like honey and soap. When she left us, she'd take even that with her. I blinked back tears, unable to persuade my feet to budge. I didn't want to see Favianne in her last moments, didn't want to remember her that way. And I sure as hell didn't want to make Zack and Cara even sadder because I couldn't hold it together.

My cell vibrated in my back pocket and I drew it out to look at the screen. If I didn't answer, my parents would worry. Or worse, they might come back, which would be bad if I'd already left town with Zack.

"I need to get this. It's my mom," I told Cara with an apologetic scrunch of my nose, then power walked back into the waiting room. "Hey, Mom. How's it going?"

"Hi, sweetie. Thought I'd check in," she replied.

My mom never "checked in." If she needed something, she'd text or e-mail or she'd show up. But she rarely called to chat and only if something was wrong.

"How's New Mexico treating you?" I asked, hoping to coax my mom into giving up whatever she needed to say.

"Good. We're all done here and getting ready to go to New Hampshire. We're swinging by to pick you up in a couple of days." Her tone sounded firm, as though I had no choice.

But I *did* have choices—possibilities my parents probably hadn't considered every time they made a hefty deposit into my account. I'd already turned eighteen and, thanks to them, I owned my Mustang outright. They'd given me a car and access to cash in case of an emergency, but in doing so, they'd also given me my freedom. She couldn't force me into anything.

"You got your way and you've been home alone for months now." Her tone held an edge that made me regret answering my phone. "You're coming with us, and we're not taking no for an answer, sweetie."

"But you promised you were staying in New

Mexico for a while." Even as the words tumbled from my lips, I reminded myself to keep my expectations low. They'd been uprooting me my whole life. Why would they settle down now?

"That was when we were trying to talk you into coming with us," she answered. "You didn't come, so your father is taking another job elsewhere. We'll try to stay in the new place longer if you like."

The job couldn't be the real reason they relocated so often. I had suspected that they weren't my real parents and that I'd been adopted—because my real mom and dad would have never kept me ignorant of being a shape-shifter—so I'd poked through their things and eventually discovered they were indeed my real parents. Which meant they had to be shape-shifters too. And in all my eighteen years, they'd never bothered to tell me I wasn't human.

Old, festered fury over their deception ignited in my brain. But with Favianne on her deathbed, I wasn't mentally equipped to go to war with my mom. "Well, have fun in New Hampshire," I said in a curt tone.

"Autumn, no. Not going to work this time. You can't blackmail us again into letting you stay. We're talking about the East Coast here. No way will we allow you to be so far away for that long. You're coming with us," she said with finality.

Oh, my God. Worst timing ever. Keeping my voice low, I spoke clearly into my cell. "I'm eighteen, Mom, so you can't make me." Especially after the ridiculously large deposits they'd made into my account.

Their desire to cover any emergency that might arise had inadvertently given me the wherewithal to keep me going for months. At least. But now was not the time to get into all that. "My boyfriend's mom is in the hospital right now dying. I'm not leaving her. I'm not leaving him either."

"You have a boyfriend? And why are you whispering?"

"Because I'm at the hospital in the waiting room. And, yes, I have a boyfriend."

A long moment ticked by before she asked, "Why didn't you tell me you had a boyfriend?"

Because my shape-shifter parents would freak over my boyfriend being a werewolf and my dating the enemy. They would never believe he wasn't like other werewolves. "Would it have changed anything?"

"Probably not. But it makes me wonder what else you're not telling me," she said.

She was one to talk! Thinking of all the ways she and my dad had deceived me made my blood boil, energizing me for a battle of wits with my mom. Yep, it was time.

CHAPTER FOUR
Autumn

"HANG ON A second." Not wanting anyone over-hearing the conversation I was about to have with my mom—and being almost desperate to get away from the smell of sickness and cleaning chemicals that my shape-shifter nose picked up all too easily—I darted through the waiting room and sailed out the exit. Outside, the streetlamps lit up the parking lot, though in a few minutes, their job would be done for the day.

I distanced myself from the building until I knew there was no one within earshot. "You mean am I keeping secrets? I don't know, Mom, am I? You're the expert on secrets."

"What? Where is this coming from, Autumn?" she asked, her words coming out cautiously.

"You had eighteen years to tell me, yet you never did. Eighteen years, Mom!" I paced—more like stomped—around the parking lot, my free hand balled into a fist.

"Tell you what?" she demanded.

"Oh, my God, Mom! You're still not going to tell me

I'm a friggin' shape-shifter?" I heard her gasp, but rage fueled me and I couldn't stop now. "Oh, and thank you *so* much for leaving me to deal with hitting maturity all on my own and letting me think there was something horribly wrong with me. Thank you *so* much for letting me agonize over whether you guys lied about being my real parents and I'd been adopted, or that I wasn't human."

As soon as I paused to get in enough air to fill my lungs—I so wasn't finished yet— my mom cut in. "Autumn, calm down."

"Don't you dare tell me to calm down. You're not the one who was lied to. And let's not forget all the time I wasted trying to prove which scenario was the correct one. I mean, I couldn't believe you'd be so negligent and not tell me I'd be morphing into a furry animal at any moment. But, no, you guys really were that deceitful!" My voice had taken on a hint of hysteria.

"Autumn, take a deep breath."

I did and it helped. But, crap, I did not need this right now. Zack was probably looking for me. Favianne might've already passed away and I hadn't said goodbye. Instead of being where Zack needed me, I was outside on a warm summer morning with sweat trickling down my back, arguing with my mom about something I couldn't change. I pinched the bridge of my nose, trying to chill out. "Why, Mom? Why didn't you tell me?"

She was silent a long moment, then sighed. "We wanted you to have a chance at a normal human life."

I clenched my teeth at the many ways I wasn't raised normally at all. "Because relocating to a new neighborhood once or twice every year and having you guys obsessively hover over me is *normal*?"

"We wanted you to be stress free for a while before you had to bear the burden of all the things that went with life as a shape-shifter."

Before the shape-shifter gene kicks in, we're exactly like humans. And while I appreciated not being burdened as a child with what my future held, some werewolves and shape-shifters hit maturity as early as fourteen. My parents should have been preparing me since then.

I scoffed. "That's your excuse? Seriously?"

"Sweetie, life as a shape-shifter... it's dangerous. And we figured the more you knew, the more stressed you'd be and the sooner you'd hit shape-shifter maturity. And then everything would change."

"I'm a teenager, Mom. Stress is my middle name. I'd already hit maturity the first time you came back and you didn't even notice."

She muttered a few choice curses. "Your father and I smoke to cover up our scent and no one suspects we're not human. I guess the smell got all over everything, including you, and kept us from sniffing you out. I'm so sorry."

"But I scrubbed down the entire house and there's been more than one werewolf around who had no idea I wasn't human."

"You've seen werewolves?" she shrieked into the phone. "How many?"

"Mom, I swear I'm not in danger. Just tell me why my scent is so light."

She waited a beat, probably wondering if she could believe I was safe. "I assume you haven't turned carnivore. Meat brings out not only our animal side but our scent too. Now tell me about the werewolves."

Right... Zack hadn't been able to detect me until I'd eaten that hamburger. "The werewolves aren't a problem, I promise."

She huffed. "There are things you don't know, important things we need to teach you. This is why you need to get here immediat—"

I cut her off. "You mean things like, oh, werewolves hate us? And that if I get caught, I could be taken as a slave, or worse, murdered?"

"Y-yes. Where did you learn all that?" she asked, her voice laced with worry.

"From Zack. My boyfriend."

"If Zack is human," she began slowly, as though she was trying to bend her mind around everything, "how does he know anything about us?"

Mom was going to lose it when I told her the truth. She'd try ten times harder to get me to go to New Hampshire. Whatever. Although Zack and I had made a pact to split up when being together become too risky, I didn't plan on sticking to that deal. I didn't want to be without him, especially right now. He was about to need me more than ever. No way would I desert him. "Because he's a werewolf," I whispered.

"A werewolf?" my mom shouted. "You must be joking. Please tell me you're not hanging out with a *werewolf.*"

"Can't. Then I'd be a liar like you." I ignored her sudden intake of air and glanced at the emergency room doors. "I have to go. Zack's mom is dying and I need to be with him. I'm sorry. I'll call you later, okay?"

"Autumn, listen to me! Being with him puts you in grave danger. Get in your car, go home, get your things, and then leave. I can meet you in Vegas or something."

"Mom, I'm staying and that's final. I can't leave him and his family. I can't." My voice broke and a sob escaped me. "I love them. I love her and Zack. I *love* him. Don't you get it?"

She was silent for a long moment. "Okay, I get it. How long does she have?"

I whimpered in an effort to control my tears. "A few hours maybe. A day at the most. I'm outside arguing with you and she's dying. I feel like the worst person in the world."

"You're not," she assured me. "But you can be compassionate while still being practical. As soon as you can, you need to pack your things and get the hell out of there. You're not safe."

I swallowed. "I know. My car's already loaded with my things, including the disposable phones you left for me. Zack's packed too. We're taking off as soon as..." I stopped, unable to say it.

"As soon as she passes?"

I squeezed my eyes shut and whispered, "Yes."

"Okay. We were prepared to come get you, but everything's different with Zack in the picture. As much as I don't want you away from us, your father and I aren't in a position just yet to travel with a were-wolf. I have a friend who owes me a favor, but you have to get to him without being followed. He'll give you both refuge for a week or two until we get there in a few days, once we're absolutely sure we won't be leading any werewolves straight to you. You'll be one hundred percent safe there with all the security he has in place. I'll text you the address."

A safe place to land sounded pretty damn good considering Zack probably wouldn't be in any kind of emotional shape to make sound decisions on where we should go. Until I knew he was back to being himself, I'd make the decisions for both of us. "Great. Send me the address and I'll be there. I promise."

"Good. As soon as we hang up, shut off your phone and text me from one of the disposables. Then I'll send you all the information."

"Okay. I gotta go." I automatically focused on the glass double doors of the hospital. I needed to get back inside. "Zack's probably looking for me."

"Speaking of Zack..."

Uh-oh, I was about to get lectured, which was the last thing I wanted at the moment since I needed to get back to Zack. But my mom had just made a huge concession by not giving me grief about him, even arranging a sanctuary for him. I could give her another minute. "What about him?"

"You're aware of the repercussions of a shape-shifter associating with a werewolf?"

"That mixing species is a big no-no? Yes. Being

with him and putting ourselves in more danger isn't the path I *want*, but I can't imagine my life without Zack. I'd rather fight for what's right than be miserable without him. Isn't that what you and Dad taught me?"

Her voice cracked on a quick laugh. "But even if you two manage to avoid the king's hunters, you'll still live a hard life, always checking over your shoulder, always afraid. Are you sure that's what you want?"

Maybe others would say I was too naïve to know true love, that I was too young to make such an important decision. But I knew what I felt when I was with Zack, and I wasn't going to give him up without a fight. "Yes."

"All right," she mumbled. "I'll support whatever decision you make. Mostly because I don't have a choice."

"Seriously?" She wasn't going to try to come between my werewolf boyfriend and me?

"If you love him, I'm sure he earned it. Drive to that address as soon as you can, and I'll see you there in a few days."

"I'll go straight to my car and text you from one of the disposables." My eyes watered. "Mom?"

"Yeah, sweetie?"

"I love you."

"Love you too. More than anything."

After hanging up, I dashed to my car, grabbed one of the phones in the emergency backpack, and texted my mom as promised. I buried the small phone in my pocket and sprinted into the building, heading straight to the waiting room. Mac and the boys had arrived, including Zack's cousin Trevor, and my best friend Maya who'd been dating Trevor.

"Where have you been?" Maya asked, circling me in her arms.

"Talking to my mom. Sorry." I released her and waved to Mac and Trevor. "Any news?"

Maya's head swayed side to side. "No."

The doors swished open and Zack approached. "Autumn, aren't you coming?"

Did I want to see Favianne all pale and thin or did I want to remember her as sunshine and sweetness? I couldn't handle being in the room with her while she lay there nearly lifeless. I wasn't sure if I could hold it together. "Trevor needs to be with her. And Mac and the boys."

"They will. Besides, it's a big room." The space between Zack's brows pinched as he sidled up to me and tangled his fingers with mine. He tugged on my hand, pulling me through the door and down the long passageway. "We don't have a lot of time."

Probably even less time than he thought. Our lives were about to change and Zack was even less ready for it than I was.

CHAPTER FIVE
—— *Zack* ——

MY MOTHER WOULDN'T be waking up. I covered her hand in mine and held tight, wishing I could breathe life into her and put off the inevitable. But I knew I couldn't stop what was about to happen.

I wanted to cry for her, for myself, for all the things we wouldn't do next week or next month, weep for all the things she wouldn't be there to share with me. I wanted someone to blame for being robbed of my mother when she was still so young, for the injustice of it all. I wanted to scream and pound on the walls, throw things and hear them crash and break. But all I could do was stand there, numb from the shock of reality.

Careful to avoid all the tubes and cords, I let go of my mom's hand and backed against the wall to give Autumn some time with her. I needed a moment to compose myself anyway.

"What should I say to her?" Autumn wiped her cheek with a fingertip and stared down at my mom's motionless form.

"I don't know." In a matter of minutes or hours,

she'd die. She'd be cremated, per her instructions, and I'd never see her again or talk to her or hug her. She'd just be gone. My face hurt from clenching my jaw. "Cara's coming back soon and the rest of the family. Whatever you need to tell her, you should do it soon." When Autumn still didn't speak, I draped an arm over her shoulder. "Do you want me to leave?"

"No." Autumn was quiet for so long I wondered if she was going to say anything else. She leaned over the bed and rested her cheek against my mom's. "Thank you so much for taking me in, making me part of your family. Thank you for being the kindest, most amazing woman I've ever known. And for giving me Zack. I..." Autumn choked on a sob before resuming. "I wish you well on your new adventure, wherever you go." There was a long pause before Autumn straightened, then added, "I love you."

I waited a beat to see if Autumn would continue, but she didn't say anything else. I planted a kiss on her cheek just as Uncle Mac, Aunt Cara, and my cousin Trevor tiptoed inside. I pulled her close, steered her back toward the wall to make room for the others, and then wrapped my arms all the way around her.

"I'm so sorry, Zack," Autumn said.

My eyes stung. I'd already said good-bye to my mother. Did I want to stay and witness as her heart pumped the last drop of blood? As much as I wanted every second with her, I didn't think I could handle a first-row seat to her life slipping away. "Me too. Let's give them some time alone with her. I need some air anyway."

Relieved to leave the suffocating room, I closed the door and led Autumn down the corridor. But as we rounded the corner, I caught a glimpse of someone in my peripheral vision. Could that have been Renzo?

Zack, Autumn directed her silent words to me, *I'm pretty sure that was Renzo. What do you think he's doing here?*

Probably keeping tabs on me. But I couldn't think about Renzo right now. I knew he probably worked for the werewolf king and he'd never allow me to go rogue, no matter how many times he'd insisted he was "on vacation." No sane werewolf would let a perfectly good recruit loose and miss out on the werewolf king's reward. I'd have to deal with Renzo at some point, but I'd work that out later.

The sun had just risen, peeking above the foothills. I drew fresh air into my lungs then turned to Autumn, the ache in my chest so unbearable I was sure I'd break. "It's like a part of me is dying."

"I know." Autumn snaked her arms around my neck and pressed her breasts against me. I took her in, the smell of her hair and the silky softness of her skin. God, what would I do without her? I maneuvered us backward until her shoulders bumped the stucco wall. I brushed my lips against hers briefly, then held her close and rested my cheek against hers.

Frustration rose up and fear, hard and ugly, devoured me. How would I go on without my mother? She'd always been there and now she was leaving me.

I was a werewolf with all the superpowers that went with it. I could leap over fences, pick up scents from across a field, and keep up with a speeding car. Yet I couldn't save my mom. I was helpless, forced to stand by and watch her fade away.

My heart missed a beat and a sudden intense sadness ravaged me. How I could feel my mom's absence from the other end of the building I had no idea, but her departure was like a car slamming into me, winding me. Moisture flowed past my lids and my limbs trembled. "She's gone. I can sense it."

Autumn released a tiny whimper as her hand stroked my back. "Me too."

"She's free now." And I was alone. I didn't want to be stoic. Just this once, I didn't want to hold back. My body vibrated and a long, agonized moan, a sound I barely recognized as mine, came from deep within me. I let go and bawled, not caring who heard me.

Although I hadn't been there when the last bit of life left her, she'd had family at her bedside. I'd already said good-bye and now, the only thing left to do was comfort my aunt, uncle, and cousins. How could I do that, though, when I was the one who needed it most?

Minutes later, Autumn was still stroking my hair, my back, my arms. "Let's go for a drive," she said. "Maybe stop and morph. You'll feel better."

I didn't answer, didn't react. Leaving my family without telling them would be horribly rude. But I'd had enough of the stench of chemicals and death, and couldn't bear to stay in the hospital another second.

"Be on alert for Renzo." Autumn took hold of my hand and guided me to her Mustang. After climbing behind the wheel, she scanned the parking lot, then retrieved her phone and powered it off. "Can I see your cell?"

I handed it to her and she shut it off. I was too numb and frozen to ask why.

"I don't know how Renzo was able to track us to Yosemite, and I don't want to take any chances." She grabbed a disposable phone, scribbled off a quick text, then tore out of the hospital parking lot and merged with traffic. A dull ache took root in my gut as I stared out the window.

Minutes later, we were on a freeway driving past buildings I didn't recognize. Before I could orient myself, she was making the circle off the 210 to get onto the 118. "I thought we were going to morph, like in the woods around our neighborhood."

"Renzo was at the hospital, remember? He'll be looking for you. I'm sorry, but we can't go back there and we can't go home."

Yeah, I'd forgotten all about that. Not only had I not been there the last moments of my mom's life, but now I was disappearing on Aunt Cara so soon after she'd lost her sister. Not to mention my uncle and cousins. Apparently there were no depths to the degree I could suck.

"I'm leaving them, just like that?" I touched my chin to my chest and rubbed my thudding temples. "I'm not even going to my own mom's funeral?"

"We can't stay there, Zack. Your mom would want

me to keep you alive and that's exactly what I intend to do." Her hands gripped the steering wheel, turning her knuckles white. "We'll call them in a few minutes. Right now we need to get some food in you and then make it to the safe house."

Safe house? "When did we plan this?"

"My mom called and I ended up telling her I knew I was a shape-shifter and that they were too. Then she insisted I get the hell out of town. I said I fully intended to, but I wasn't leaving without you. So she gave me an address of an old friend who owes her a favor." Autumn checked her review mirror before glancing over her shoulder and switching lanes.

I nodded woodenly, vaguely wondering if the friend's favor included providing refuge for a were-wolf. If so, Autumn had to have told her mother about me. But I had no desire to push for details. I'd lost my parents, my extended family, and soon I'd lose Autumn. That was inevitable. What was the point in fighting for a few more days with her when I was going to end up alone anyway?

We'd already learned the hard way what she risked by associating with me. If she'd never met me, she wouldn't have been taken hostage by her werewolf ex-boyfriend, and she wouldn't have been nearly killed by the werewolf assigned to monitor me. And Renzo wouldn't be one more werewolf whose motives were a mystery and who could turn on us at any moment.

If I'd left her alone from the beginning and ignored her, she would've never fallen for me and her risk of being discovered would be dramatically decreased. I didn't care how tolerant Renzo seemed to be of our relationship. I suspected it was an act. At the very least, he was hiding something, I was sure of it. And that secret could get both Autumn and me killed. All because I was a werewolf.

If Autumn and I separated, she wouldn't be by herself; she'd meet up with her shape-shifter parents. Which was where she belonged. I needed to think of her needs now, not my own. But with the loss of my mom so raw and fierce, the thought of being without Autumn was more than I could bear. I hoped this weak moment on my part wouldn't be the biggest mistake of my life.

CHAPTER SIX

──── *Autumn* ────

WE WERE TEN minutes into our drive and it was well past breakfast time. Zack and I hadn't eaten since dinner the night before and hunger clawed its way out of my belly and into my veins. Zack hadn't mentioned wanting food, but he had to be starving. I didn't need him getting low blood sugar and then his mind veering off into even darker and scarier places.

A sign ahead off the 405 freeway read *Harold's Diner*. That was good enough for me. I took the next exit and turned into the restaurant parking lot. After one last scan to make sure I didn't see any midnight blue Jaguars—or any other signs of Renzo—I scrambled out of the car and went around to Zack's side. When I opened the passenger door, he stared blankly up at me. I tipped my head toward the restaurant entrance. "We should refuel since we may not have another chance for a while."

As he clambered out of the passenger side, the empty look in his eyes seemed to have taken up permanent residence. My heart ached for him, but I couldn't let his pain distract me. I had to get us to safety. Looping my arm through his, I directed him toward our next meal.

Inside the restaurant, he sat silently in the booth by the window and gazed out, his arms dangling at his sides. When the server came to take our order, he didn't glance her way at all, just continued his staring contest with the glass that separated us from outside. When it became clear he wasn't going to answer the server, I ordered him a burger.

Our food arrived and his burger still sat uneaten minutes later. I wolfed down a good portion of my pasta, enough to keep me from fainting of hunger, then switched to Zack's side of the booth and scooted close to him. I grabbed the burger with both hands and lifted it to his mouth. "Take a bite, Zack. You need to eat while you can."

With wooden movements, he relieved me of the burger. He ate painfully slow, but he kept going and that was all I cared about. When he finished the last bite, I relaxed against the seat. Through the restaurant window, I examined the parking lot again for Renzo's midnight blue Jaguar, but I didn't see anything remotely similar. I fished in my purse for the disposable cell and dialed Maya's number.

She answered on the first ring. "Hello?"

"It's me," I said, remembering that she wouldn't recognize the number of the new phone.

"Where are you? You two disappeared and... she's

gone, Autumn." Maya squeaked out a sob.

"I know." I hiccupped, wiping away a tear. "How's Trevor and everyone else?"

"Not great, but they're dealing." She sniffed. "What about Zack?"

"Not so good." I cast him a glance, suspecting he'd forgotten I existed. He was staring at the napkin he'd left crumpled beside his plate. "His family needs him right now, but... he's pretty torn up. I'm getting him out of town."

Maya asked where we were going and when we'd be back, but I kept my answers vague and promised to call her in a few days.

Zack and I piled back into my Mustang. I resumed GPS, which directed me back onto the 405. A few minutes later, before I steered the Mustang onto the 101 north, traffic slowed and I snuck a peek at Zack. His hands covered his face and his shoulders quaked. I wanted to comfort him, but I forced my focus back to the road.

Obeying my GPS, I got off the freeway in Calabasas. Zack looked a little better by then, slightly less like a zombie. Maybe the recent sob-fest had done him some good.

We'd entered a neighborhood with beautifully trimmed mature trees lining the street. The huge houses were spread out, each with long, winding driveways and surrounded by lushly green, perfectly manicured grounds.

"Your destination is on your right," my phone informed me after another mile and several more gorgeous mansions.

I pulled up to the intricate wrought iron gates, my eyes glued to the chateau-style structure with its spires and steeply pitched roof. It was massive, big enough to be a hotel and by far, the biggest house we'd passed. I rolled down the window to depress the button at the intercom.

"May I help you?" a female voice with a British accent asked from the small square box.

"I'm here to see, uh..." I glanced down at my phone to double-check my mom's text, hoping I was at the correct place. "Cedric Gallagher. He should be expecting me."

Any idea who this Cedric guy is? Zack asked. It was the first time he'd uttered a word, aloud or otherwise, since I'd told him we weren't going back to the hospital. Or home.

"You may enter. Please bring your car all the way to the end of the driveway and someone will meet you," the female voice said.

I rolled up the window and accelerated when the gate began to slide over. Which end of the driveway? It was almost as wide as it was long. Like a freakin' mall parking lot. "No, I don't know anything about Cedric, but my mom wouldn't send me anywhere unless she was one hundred percent sure we'd be safe."

The Mustang glided along the smooth stone driveway and an enormous structure to the left of the mansion came into view. The garage maybe? Zack had worked at an auto shop for a while and had fixed my car on occasion. The way Zack ogled it now, he was probably betting it housed some pretty cool cars.

As we drew nearer to the mansion, not a soul was in sight. If anyone was around, they certainly kept well hidden.

"There's something... something different about this place." Zack studied the row of hedges that merged with a clump of trees, then stared at the building a long moment. "Just don't know what."

Well good. I preferred Zack on alert. Maybe this meant he was back, some part of him at least. I had Cedric Gallagher and his "different" environment to thank for it.

As soon as I opened the driver's side door, I felt it. A strange energy not unlike my own, but definitely not shape-shifter or werewolf. What the hell were these people?

Zack arrived at my side and laced his fingers through mine as someone dropped from the roof—which was four stories up—and landed in front of us with a thud. My ribs tensed and we took an instinctive step back.

The man's lip curled up, exposing long white fangs. "Werewolves."

I didn't correct him on the plural part. Better if he had no clue I was a shape-shifter who was consorting with a werewolf. My mother may have had faith in Cedric, but that didn't mean we were safe from everyone else he associated with. Any one of them could turn us in for a reward. "We're here to see Cedric Gallagher," I said.

His dark blond hair skittered over his forehead when he folded his arms over his muscular chest.

"For what purpose?"

I inhaled again, caught the sweet metallic scent, and it hit me. What other life form could smell so strongly of blood? *Vampires*, I told Zack silently. From what little I'd read in the books Zack's father had left for him, vampires hated werewolves.

In daylight? This is not good, he said.

Yeah, like I didn't already realize that.

CHAPTER SEVEN
—— *Autumn* ——

ZACK GRIPPED MY hand as we stood in front of the mansion—more like palace—and watched the vampire. *Not liking this, Autumn. We shouldn't be here.*

Would you rather Renzo or some other werewolf finds us?

I don't know. My gut wants to trust your mom's friend, but I don't think I should rely on my instinct today.

My instinct's not much more dependable than yours. I'd had a hellish day too, and I'd been totally wrong about my ex-boyfriend Daniel and my ex-best friend Gina. *But this is our only option and my mom promised we'd be safe.*

Zack shrugged. *Okay.*

"For what purpose?" the vampire repeated, a low hiss emanating from him.

I raised my chin. "Cedric is expecting me."

The vampire scowled. "He invited werewolves into his home? Unlikely."

"Ask him yourself," I replied, sounding much tougher than I felt. "I'm Autumn and this is Zack."

He deliberated for several seconds, regarding each of us doubtfully. "Tony," he said, his eyes flaring.

Zack and Tony exchanged man nods and the scent of testosterone thickened.

"So is he here?" I asked in an effort to slice through the tension.

A thick heavy door under a stone archway swung open and a beautiful black girl with long curly hair came into view. "C'mon then. He's consented to meet with the wolves," she said in that same British accent.

Tony's brows flew up. "He has?"

"Apparently our sovereign's secrets never end," the girl said dryly.

Sovereign? Did that mean Cedric was their leader? King? I offered a friendly smile. "I'm Autumn and this is Zack." I hitched a thumb at him.

She shot us a scalding look. "And I don't care." She whirled around and disappeared through the arched doorway.

Zack and I glanced at each other before following her into an enclosed courtyard. Light streamed in from zillions of glass squares arching toward the middle of the ceiling to form a dome, showering sunshine onto a heavenly scented green garden bursting with colorful blooms.

But I didn't get a chance to truly enjoy the visual feast because she made a hard right, leading us through a door that took us inside. As soon as Zack shut the door after us, the vampire circled around. "I'm told that not only will I welcome you into our home, but I must be your tour guide as well. Your host feels that if you are left to your own devices, you should be able to find your way about." Her mouth twisted in disgust before she turned her back on us and resumed walking.

"This is the waiting room." She waved a hand to encompass the area as she continued her brisk pace. Through another doorway the lighting dimmed, but I could still see a couple of pool tables, several booths lining the wall, a dartboard and a stage in the corner with a standing microphone tucked to the side. "Which opens into the game room, which leads to the club and, finally," she walked quickly past a sprinkling of tables, "the café."

And beyond that, I spied the kitchen. "Do vampires eat actual food or is this just for show?"

As if I hadn't uttered a word, she pivoted to the left and led the way into another room. "This is the theater and through that door, the chapel." She made another sharp left. "This way to the gym."

A sign above a door with steamy windows announced a sauna and beside it, a long window with a pool on the other side. We breezed by it to arrive in front of an enormous room with exercise equipment of every kind—elliptical, weights, treadmills, and even punching bags filled the room. With enough space for a large, matted area that I guessed was for sparring or combat training.

At the far end of the room, we passed through another door that returned us to the atrium, except now we were on the opposite side from where we'd entered.

"And this is where we began." She spun, pushed through yet another door, and climbed a plush staircase.

"We'll skip the second floor, which consists of offices and such. Can't imagine him involving werewolves in our affairs," she muttered, turning up the next flight and exiting through the door of the third floor. A few yards farther, our path snaked into a mezzanine. My eyes devoured the chandelier overhead and the hundreds of tiny teardrop crystals.

I slowed across the corridor and past the old tapestries on the wall that smelled of age and dust. I tried to imagine the texture of the fringe if I were to let the thin strands slip between my fingers. But I kept my hands to my side as the scent of oil from huge, gold-framed paintings wafted up my nose. Sculptures stood on blocks at both ends of the hall and above me the thick crown moldings accented the high ceilings.

"This floor is the staff quarters. Not our final destination."

Yet we followed her through the entire length of it, same route as downstairs, around the center that had a railing and afforded a view of the courtyard and the glorious perfume of the blooms below. We passed rooms: a lounge, another game room, kitchen and café, laundry facilities, and, finally, more bedrooms. At the other end, we trailed after her up another staircase. "The fourth floor is the king's suites where he keeps several rooms, along with his council."

Kayla paused at a door at the top of the stairs,

and placed her hand over a glass plate on the wall. After two clicks, she opened the door and waved us through, then closed and locked it behind us.

Now my mom's confidence in Cedric's security made sense.

This floor was similar to the one below—it had its own kitchen and laundry facilities, as well as a lounge and game room. I wondered how humans put up with such gigantic houses and how long it could take to get from one end to the other. Since they didn't have the stamina of a werewolf or vampire, they'd need a good intercom system and staff to fetch. Of course anyone who owned a place like this could afford anything they wanted.

Just like before, Kayla paused at another door and knocked before placing her hand over a glass plate. After a click, she opened the door and motioned us inside.

She pointed to the part of the room covered by an enormous rug. On top of it, two overstuffed chairs sat in front of a wide, glossy mahogany desk with an impossible amount of fancy carvings. My feet sank into the velvety threads of the rug, and I felt guilty for still wearing shoes.

As soon as we sat, she glared down at us. Yep, a nice, friendly vampire welcome. Awesome.

Maybe this wasn't such a good idea, Zack told me.

Anything that brought Zack back from the dead had to be a great idea. This Zack was way better than the zombie I'd spent most of the day with. But whether we were with hostile vampires or not, I didn't believe this Cedric guy would harm us. *No way would my mom send us here with even the smallest chance something could happen to me.*

The woman pursed her full lips. "Anyone ever tell you how rude it is to speak telepathically in front of others?" she snapped.

"Kayla, is that any way to treat my guests?" A tall man with ginger hair wore a charcoal-gray suit that fit his big frame perfectly. He strode into the room, quickly closing the distance between us, and I immediately caught the pungent smell of blood. Another vampire.

Kayla bowed. "You granted them entry, but I assumed you weren't aware they were werewolves."

"Otherwise they wouldn't be here?" Cedric asked. "I'm fully cognizant of their genetic composition. Now please spread the word that these werewolves are not to be harmed. They are under my protection."

"From other werewolves?" Her eyes shifted between Cedric and us. "Knowing the werewolf king, they'll probably get killed anyway once they leave."

My chest tightened with that little glimpse into my future. Always running. Always in danger of being discovered and killed.

"Or maybe these two will surprise us," Cedric continued. "Maybe if we can keep them safe, one day they'll overthrow the werewolf king." His head whipped around to Kayla at her amused cough.

I agreed with Kayla; that was some dream. Zack and I weren't warriors and we were a long way from being able to protect ourselves, much less take over an entire body of government.

"But are you sure keeping werewolves in the palace would be wise?" Kayla asked. "With the unrest among—"

"They are guests in our home and will be treated as such. That will be all, Kayla," he said in a firm, yet kind tone.

"Yes, sir." Keeping her head down, she slunk away and left the way we came.

"My suite is soundproofed, so you can speak freely." Cedric took a seat behind his desk, then steepled his fingers and studied us.

I took in the rest of the room—the ridiculously elaborate green drapes and valance, complete with gold ropes and tassels. And then there was the gorgeous grandfather clock—etched glass panels covered most of the front and exposed the wheels and other mechanisms. I could swear the metal parts looked like they were made of gold. Probably cost more than my car.

Cedric cleared his throat. "As you can see, a wolf's presence puts me in an uncomfortable position. Your mother's timing couldn't be worse."

"Why is that?" Zack cast a worried glance my way.

"It happens that a couple of our best men were attacked a few weeks ago in Scottsdale, Arizona. By werewolves." Cedric growled. "Lacking a cure for werewolf bite, they died and my people are in an uproar."

"Rogue werewolves?" Zack asked.

"We thought so at first but then it happened again in Montana. Whether they're the same werewolves or not, we can't be sure until we get more intel."

Uh-oh. The incidents happened first in Arizona, then in Montana? "My parents were in both those places the past couple of weeks. Except my mom and dad aren't werewolves, so they couldn't have been the ones who bit your men." Still, I couldn't ignore the timing.

"Right. Both your parents are shape-shifters, of course." Cedric regarded me for several beats, as if he were measuring his next words. "I find it intriguing they were in the same place at the same time of the murders, though. I'll get in touch with your mother and see if she knows anything that may help us locate those responsible."

Fear gripped my heart and wouldn't let go. "You don't think they had anything to do with it, do you?"

"Absolutely not." He reached a hand out and laid it on my wrist. "But she may have some insight as to why my men are being attacked."

"So... you're not sure if they're isolated instances or—" Zack began before being cut off.

"Or if I'm at war without the courtesy of a formal declaration." Cedric's jaw clenched.

"Should we... leave?" I asked.

"It would certainly be easier on me." He stared vacantly, lost in thought as he thrummed his fingers on the surface of his polished desk. "Years ago, your mother was of great service, saved my life, in fact. I told her to call upon me if she were ever in need. I can't disregard that obligation."

"But do you think we're at risk if we stay here?" Zack asked Cedric before glancing at me—probably wondering if anywhere else would be better.

"I can keep you safe." Cedric leaned back in his overstuffed chair, the leather creaking as his large shoulders shoved against it. "There's a fully-stocked kitchen down the hall and with over twenty thousand square feet on this floor, it's unlikely we'll get in each other's way until your parents come for you next week. You'll have to stay here in my personal suite, though, since security is significantly higher—in case any vampires decide to take revenge on you two because of the recent deaths. I have two extra rooms." He pointed to a door on one side of his study next to the door leading to the corridor, then aimed a thumb on the opposite side toward two doors. "You're welcome to one of them."

He moved to get up, then sat back down and scratched his chin thoughtfully. "Probably best if we don't mention to your parents that I let you share a room."

"Deal." Wow, we'd get to stay together in a private suite of a grand estate. I could live with that. Swiveling, I faced Zack. "Seems better than the alternative."

"It's settled." Cedric pointed to the single door closest to the hallway. "That's your room. One thing though." He leaned over his desk toward us and glanced around for eavesdroppers.

Icy tingles crawled up my neck. By the look on his face, this had to be serious.

"Most vampires have gone their whole lives without meeting a shape-shifter. They wouldn't know the difference between you and a werewolf. I doubt you two are stupid enough to mix species, but anyone in the palace could turn you in to the were- wolf king for being involved in any way at all. This place would be crawling with werewolves trying to kill you for that transgression." Cedric pinned me with a stare. "I'll do whatever I can to protect you, but don't make my job harder than it needs to be. Keep close to Zack. Since your scent is unusually weak, they'll pick up on only werewolf and the likeli- hood of them sniffing you out is slim."

"Yes, sir," I answered, hoping my cover wouldn't be blown.

"I'll send Kayla up in a moment to escort you to the car for your things. In the meantime, have a look around."

"I think I might." I walked to the window. Holy smokes, the view was spectacular. Trees as far as I could see. "How many acres are yours?"

Cedric halted and turned. "About a hundred."

Oh, that was a lot. I couldn't wait to run through the forest later. "This place is enormous. I had no idea houses like this existed in California."

"We finished building last year and we've been quiet about it. We're trying to stay off the radar, you understand."

"I'd probably feel the same way." Zack nodded. "But maybe living in a less conspicuous house would draw less attention."

"I prefer to keep my court nearby, as well as my staff." Cedric rested against the wall, his mouth curving as if our questions amused him. "Safety in numbers."

"How many vampires live here?" I asked.

Cedric tapped his chin. "Close to thirty, I believe."

"And they all have a grudge against werewolves?" Zack asked.

Cedric grunted. "Good point. I'll send Tony along when you get your things."

Great, we'd be guarded by two vamps we already knew were hostile toward us.

Zack stood. "We feel safer by the second," he said in a deadpan tone.

Cedric pushed off the wall and headed toward the door. "My people wouldn't dare cross me. And how much trouble could you cause by going to your car and back?"

"We're not worried about the trouble *we* might cause," Zack muttered after Cedric disappeared out the door. Zack tugged on my hand. "Let's get this over with."

As soon as we reached the doorway, Kayla reappeared. "Let's be off then."

We shadowed her through the endless corridor and down the stairs, the awkward silence grating on my nerves. How could we stay in a vampire lair knowing they all hated us? I had to at least try to build some sort of trust. The only way I could think of to accomplish that was to engage her in conversation and let things happen naturally.

I picked up speed so I could walk beside Kayla. "So what do you do here?"

She continued at a brisk pace, staring straight ahead. "Security. But I also train any newly turned vampires in battle."

I would've loved to get in on some of that training, but the chances of Kayla teaching her enemy to win a fight were probably pretty slim. "How long have you worked for Cedric?"

When Tony fell into step beside us, Kayla didn't break her stride. "Hundred years or so," she answered.

I flinched. "Seriously? I couldn't imagine holding down the same job for one year, much less a hundred."

She held the door open to the outside and a part of me wondered why she was sending us out first. I gulped. Together we proceeded ahead and into the sunlight of the atrium—which we already knew didn't bother some vampires at all. Damn. I hoped Kayla and Tony would be enough to hold off the vamps if we were swarmed.

A buzzing sound reached my ears and I went on alert. Zack shielded me as several blurry forms advanced. Three vampires—a female and two males—stopped a mere two feet away, still as statues, their gazes locked on Zack and me. The female vampire hissed.

Kayla hovered in front of us, her arms stretched backward like we were in her protective bubble. "They are under the king's protection. No harm will come to them while they are under his roof," she warned, her voice taking on a menacing tone.

I should've been comforted knowing we had support from the top of the food chain. But the three threatening vamps in front of me were yanking on my safety net.

Tony slipped into the space between Kayla and the

vampires. "Amy, Michael, Gustavo, His Majesty has his reasons for providing sanctuary for these wolves. You will not dare defy King Cedric."

Amy took a step back, never taking her eyes off us, and then she motioned the two others to follow. They vanished, melting into the wooded area behind the house.

Zack's breath rushed from his lungs as soon as the vampires were out of our line of vision. "Thank you."

Kayla shot us each a stern look. "In obeying our king, Tony and I have betrayed our own people. You'd better prove worthy or I'll suck you dry myself. Now grab your things and let's get the hell back to the king's suite."

Note to self: Don't wander the estate without Kayla and Tony. I hoped they'd be guarding us every second.

† † †

"I don't know why we're bothering to unpack." Zack stuffed the last of his things in the bottom drawer of the chest and whirled around to face me. "They hate us. Even the vampires protecting us don't want us here. How long before Cedric and Kayla give up and decide it's easier to let the whole household feed on us?"

After shooting off a quick text to my mom to let her know we'd arrived safely, I powered off the phone and tossed it on the bed. "Let's give it some time. We might end up here longer than a few days and we don't want to live out of a suitcase. May as well be comfortable." I leaned a hip along the front of the dresser. "And even if Cedric decides he doesn't want to risk alienating his people, wouldn't he make some kind of effort to get us out of here safely?"

"Safely to where?" Zack hadn't budged from where he'd been standing in front of his dresser, his eyes holding an empty stare. "The werewolf king knows about me. I'm expected to show up on his doorstep any day. He'll send someone after me if I don't. And then there's always Renzo. Nowhere is safe."

I crossed the room and let my knuckles caress his jaw, but he still didn't seem to see me. "We expected this, Zack. It's not a big surprise."

His unfocused gaze drifted to somewhere behind me. "We've killed a scout and Renzo knows about it. Fraternizing with the enemy brings the death penalty, and Renzo knows we're together. We have no idea why he hasn't turned us in, but it's only a matter of time before someone nails us." He stepped away and ran his hands through his hair.

None of that was news to me and shouldn't have been news to Zack either. Maybe his negativity had more to do with having doubts about being with me. "We were always going to be on the run, Zack." I peeked at him as he paced the room. The whites around his deep green irises were bloodshot.

"Yeah, I know." He scrubbed his hands over his face. "It's been a hard day."

"I wish I could undo the entire morning. Maybe things won't seem so bleak after some sleep." Today had been long and brutal for me too, and I wanted more than anything to wipe it all away and get lost in Zack's hands on me, his thumbs digging into my hips. But he'd been through too much these past few hours and I didn't want to push. For now, he needed rest. I could use some of that too.

His gaze raked over me, from the brown military boots on my feet to the snug jeans and then up to my V-neck tee. Since I finally had his attention, I closed the distance and snaked my arms around his neck. He brushed his fingers across my cheek. "I don't know what I'd do without you," he said, barely above a whisper.

"Ditto." Sliding my hand down his shoulder, I gently took his hand and coaxed him toward the bed. I stopped when the backs of my knees bumped the mattress. "C'mon. We should get some rest."

Zack's palm rested at my hip as he touched his forehead to mine. His eyes smoldered and my lungs tightened like they were sealing shut. "You're so beautiful," he said.

I absorbed his words, allowing them to cocoon me, and waited for what he might do next. And then his mouth was on mine, laying waste to any inclination I may have had to hold back.

God, he hadn't kissed me all day. "I've missed you," I rasped when he came up for air.

"Not as much as I missed you." He lowered his mouth to mine again, then he picked me up by my hips and I wrapped my legs against his waist. My back collided with the mattress, our hands in a frenzy for each other, our mouths hungry. My chest heaved, my heart pounding.

A rumble began deep in Zack's throat before he rolled off me. He tunneled his hands through his hair. "It's too easy to get carried away with you."

"Likewise," I said in an unsteady voice as I curled up against him.

A long moment later, he reached for my hand then whispered, "I'm scared. Of being without my mom, my family." He leaned over to land a kiss on the top of my head. "You."

"But we're together now. We don't have to think about the future yet." I inhaled, absorbing his musky scent. The strain of the day had worn on me too. Snuggled up to him, I drifted off to sleep, but remained on the edge of consciousness. Just because I'd tried to ease Zack's worry by insisting my mother wouldn't have sent us anywhere dangerous didn't mean I believed we were totally safe. I only knew that my mom believed it.

CHAPTER EIGHT
—— *Zack* ——

THE SUN HAD set and our room was almost pitch black. I reached into my pocket to grab my cell to check the time, hoping we hadn't slept until the next morning. As hard as my stomach was yowling for food, I wouldn't have been surprised. But only three hours had passed.

I peered over at Autumn through the dark, easily finding the line of her jaw with my superhuman vision, her long black lashes, the way her thick brown hair fanned over the pillow, and her slightly parted full lips. Memories of our pre-nap kiss hijacked me and all I could think about was doing it again.

But I'd made her carry the brunt of my burden earlier, which made me reluctant to wake her. The idea that I'd made things harder for her than they needed to be had my chest aching. I'd make it up to her somehow.

Maybe I'd wake her after all.

I maneuvered myself over her, pressing my weight into her soft, warm body. Her lids fluttered, exposing her big brown eyes, and she reached over to run her fingers up my spine. She moaned and the urge to touch every inch of her overruled all logic. When my thumb grazed her breast, she took in a quick lungful of air and kissed me harder as her legs molded against my thighs.

Her sweet taste invaded my senses and everything else around me dimmed. All I knew was her: the warmth of her skin at my fingertips, the curve of her waist against my palm, the way her hips followed me as we swallowed each other's whispers with every kiss.

I reached for the button of her jeans. She gasped and blocked me. "What are you doing?"

Trying to get her naked.

Oh, hell. Not that I was opposed to having every inch of her silky, exposed skin against me, but I couldn't actually have sex with her. We couldn't get remotely close to doing that. Not if we wanted to stay strong to be able to protect ourselves.

Werewolves and shape-shifters weren't supposed to interact in any way. Period. Not just because it was illegal, but also because it wasn't safe. Legend said that mixing species caused both species to lose their supernatural abilities. If we gave in to our desires, we'd be too weak to protect ourselves later. Like Hannah and Eli who escaped from the werewolf king centuries ago and hadn't been seen since. Even if they survived the king's henchmen—highly improbable—they'd most likely mixed species and were long since buried. Until we discovered otherwise, Autumn and I could never do much more than kiss.

That I'd let it get this far and nearly lost control was bad. Especially considering we were right smack in the middle of an awful lot of hostile vamps where we needed our strength the most. I abandoned her zipper, sighed, and rested my cheek against hers. "I hate this."

"Not more than I do." She stroked the back of my arms and it felt nice. Really nice. God, I wanted to do all the things to her I'd been fantasizing about for months. That would keep us in bed for a few days.

I needed to refuel, but working off my extra energy might take my mind off Autumn's unbelievable body. Or not. It was worth a try.

"I need to morph." I groaned and rolled off her. "I hope the vampire king has as much control over his subjects as he thinks he does." My feet touched the ground and I held my hand out for her.

She let me pull her up. "Since he's all we got, I hope so."

"Remember what Cedric said and stay close to me so they don't catch your scent. Or lack thereof," I whispered. "Wolf form only, okay?"

"Roger that." She kissed me on the nose and tugged me toward the door.

We vacated our room, which led us to Cedric's study where we'd met with him earlier. He glanced up from the monitor squinting, surrounded by a mountain of paperwork.

"You don't have assistants to do that for you?"

Autumn wrinkled her nose.

Cedric mumbled something but I couldn't be sure if they were even words. "Usually, yes," he said. "But I have some investments and concerns that I see to personally. Off for a run?" The king clearly understood werewolves' compulsion to morph daily.

"Unless you don't mind if I hang around here and destroy the place." In my wolf form I was pretty big since I stayed the same weight when I changed shape. Minimally, the slick hardwood floors could get scratched by the long claws of a nearly two-hundred-pound werewolf. The carpeted sections would get shredded.

The king's eyes danced in amusement. "Kayla and Tony will be here any moment."

Autumn angled her head. "So she'll escort us everywhere we go?"

Cedric hiked up one brow. "Would you rather risk being attacked by an angry mob of blood suckers?"

Autumn shook her head. "That came out wrong. I meant, well, you're going through an awful lot of trouble and—"

"And after you leave, I'll *still* be indebted to your mother. She saved my life. I'm merely providing a temporary safe house for her daughter and boyfriend."

The king definitely sounded committed. But could we trust him? Didn't they eat humans? Probably werewolves too. "So, um, I hate to ask the obvious. Do vampires—"

"Yes, we prefer to drink human blood." He glanced up from the monitor again. "No, it doesn't have to be fresh and straight from the vein. We can do frozen blood or take it in bags if we need to. Yes, we can sustain ourselves on animal blood, though it's not nearly as tasty," he rattled off as if he'd been asked about his diet a million times before.

"Right." Autumn blinked.

"I've already notified Kayla you two need to go out." He aimed an index finger at his head. He'd told her by telepathy, of course.

A tap sounded at the door. It cracked open and Kayla's head popped through. "We'll be waiting outside."

"Off with you then." King Cedric resumed squinting at the monitor, which was immediately followed by profanity.

"You need help?" Autumn inched toward the huge wooden desk. "I'm pretty good with computers."

Scowling, he leaned back in his chair. "Not unless you're an expert at getting the columns to add up on this spreadsheet."

Autumn shot him a smug look, rounded the desk, and nudged him out of her way. "Child's play. Which column?"

"I need the total right there." He pointed at a field.

Autumn's fingers tap-danced across the keyboard. A moment later, she straightened. "When you have a *real* computer problem, let me know."

He studied her a moment. "What else can you do?"

"Website design, a little programming. I'm Photoshop certified."

"You're hired."

Autumn laughed. "I can't accept your money, but it'd be great to have something to take my mind off all the vampires wishing we were dead."

"And if you have any cars that need fixing, you only need to show me the way," I added. "We're happy to help any way we can... under the condition that we get fed soon."

The king's eyes sparkled. "Today's my lucky day. As it turns out, the Bentley developed a humming noise yesterday. The kitchen on this floor was fully stocked in anticipation of your arrival, so go ahead and raid it when you're ready."

Relief washed over me. If we're helping in some way, we wouldn't be sponging off the vampires. They might even see that we weren't all that bad. "I'll check out the Bentley tomorrow after breakfast."

"Fine. Have a good run, but don't wander too far from Kayla and Tony. Just because we've got a hundred acres doesn't mean you need to explore all of it tonight."

I saluted the king and we headed out. Kayla threw me a strange look and I wondered if she'd been eavesdropping.

"Tony will be here any moment," Kayla said. "We should wait for him."

"Okay." Autumn seemed relieved. As much as she insisted we were safe with her mom's friend, I doubted she was completely convinced.

"The others won't be won over so easily." Kayla folded her arms over her chest, her mouth drawn.

"If ever. It's been a rough few weeks and a werewolf bite is a horrible way to die. We may have many advantages over werewolves, but you have the ultimate weapon. They won't forget that anytime soon."

My dad had left me a pile of books. I'd read every one on werewolves and the pamphlet from Shape-shifter Werewolf Alliance Against Slavery and Tyranny, but at the time, I'd been fixated on learning about werewolves and had only skimmed the books on shape-shifters, witches, and vampires.

"What are your advantages?" I leaned against the wall, trying to act casual about pumping her for information.

"If a day comes that I fully trust you, I'll have no problem telling you anything you want to know." Her dark eyes told me I wouldn't hear about those advantages anytime soon, not from her.

"I love your hair." Autumn stepped away from me to get a closer look at Kayla. "It's so black and shiny. Gorgeous."

I wondered if she was trying to soften Kayla up. But Autumn wasn't the type to kiss up to someone to get what she wanted. She was usually nice to everyone and if she needed something from someone she didn't care for, she'd work out another way to get it. There wasn't an insincere bone in her body.

"Thanks." Kayla's twitching lip told me we were one step closer to getting that information.

"What is this?" Tony's mouth twisted. "Fraternizing with the dogs?"

Kayla's gaze averted in guilt, and I knew we'd lost our miniscule progress. But whatever. So long as they were loyal to the king, we were safe. From them anyway. I wasn't so sure about the twenty-something others in the palace.

CHAPTER NINE
—— *Zack* ——

OUR PAWS COVERED only a fraction of the king's acres of woods. After the long day, we craved that release more than usual and ran hard. But having freedom to roam such a large chunk of property gave us a false sense of safety. We'd stayed out longer than planned, and I was beginning to feel antsy.

Where are Kayla and Tony? I asked Autumn. *They were around a minute ago.*

Dunno. I'm nervous about being so far from them, Autumn replied.

I slid to a stop and sniffed the air. *They're close by. I can smell 'em.*

Yeah, but I smell someone else too, Autumn told me, her nose high in the air.

Crap. So did I. My heart banged against my ribs. *We'd better head back.*

Autumn took off and I followed. I considered howling to get Kayla to come to us, but that could signal every other vampire too.

In my peripheral vision, a shadow flashed toward

us and rammed into Autumn. She yipped and crashed to the ground. After bouncing up, she huddled with me against the nearly unseen force, our furry butts meeting so we had each other's backs.

Cedric said a werewolf bite kills, so they'll try to avoid our teeth, I reminded Autumn. Except she wasn't a werewolf, which meant her bite wasn't deadly and she had no weapon against them. They didn't know that though.

Another shadow advanced, and I snarled and snapped. But the vamp was too fast and I could only tear its pant leg. Two new shapes raced toward us, but we were ready, our teeth exposed. Four against two. Great.

Maybe we should make a run for it, Autumn suggested as the vamps hurled themselves at us repeatedly.

They're faster than we are. Kayla and Tony should be here any second. I hoped. These guys weren't able to get past our jaws to do any damage, but we couldn't hold them off forever. We'd have to do something soon.

Unless Kayla and Tony helped plan the ambush, she said.

In that case, we were on our own. The vampires slowed and backed up, circling us. "Why are you here?" a tall, blond man asked.

Adrenaline roared through my body. *They're stopping to chat, hoping to catch us off guard.* I growled, making my fangs appear as big and scary as possible. *Don't let them distract you. And make sure they can't get close to any part of you except your teeth. We can stall them for a while.*

"Were you sent to kill us?" The blond man led the others in a circle, trapping us. As he passed Autumn and neared me, he commanded, "Testify, wolves! Tell us why you're in vampire territory."

I lunged, my fangs sinking into his side. He snarled and struggled, but my teeth burrowed deeper then scraped across his abdomen. He drove a fist into my back, knocking me away. I took some of his flesh with me. He dove at Autumn and his fangs latched onto her neck. Before I could rip him apart, Autumn managed to claw him off her.

Two vamps advanced on me but backed away when I advanced on them teeth first. The blond one stumbled away while we repositioned our bodies to cover each other and waited for another opportunity to strike one of them.

Are you okay? I asked Autumn.

Yeah, he didn't get much blood. Don't worry about me. Just concentrate on biting the next one.

My hot girlfriend was also a cutthroat. I would've been more amused by that if our lives hadn't been at stake.

"You'll die here, dogs." The blond vamp laughed.

Maybe, maybe not. But I bit you, leech, so your death is guaranteed, I thrust at him telepathically.

He sneered. "Yes, you did, but werewolf blood is the cure. I'll be healed in a matter of moments."

He'd heard me talk to him silently. Which meant the king could probably hear me too. *Your Majesty, we're being attacked in the woods. Something must've happened to Kayla and Tony, because I haven't seen them for several minutes.*

While making sure I knew Autumn's position behind me, I kept track of the blond vamp in front of me. I directed my next silent words to all four vampires. *Your king is on his way.*

The other three vampires vanished, leaving the blond one alone.

Werewolf blood is the cure? I asked.

He smirked. Of course he'd be cocky, since he believed he already had the cure. I heard a *whoosh!* and an instant later, Cedric stood in front of us. Tony and Kayla flanked him, both with blood stains over their hearts. A pungent metallic scent wafted up my nose.

My gaze transferred to the blond vamp, but he'd taken off. I shifted into my human form, thankful that Autumn had talked me into wearing all natural fibers that morphed with me. I didn't usually mind being suddenly buck naked and having to fish around for my clothes, but this time I was grateful for not having to.

"Did you see any of them?" Autumn asked, slightly out of breath.

"No." King Cedric folded his arms over his chest. "Explain to me what happened."

"We were on our way back and something struck me. Next thing I knew, we were surrounded by four vampires," Autumn said, and then turned to Kayla. "What happened to you guys?"

"Someone staked us. They were so fast we couldn't identify who." She scanned the grounds. "Would you be able describe them?"

"We were too busy trying not to die and it's dark out here," I said. "A redheaded woman, but she didn't show us her face. And a couple of guys. The blond man stopped to talk so we got a pretty good look at him. Taller than me and bulky. He's wearing a black T-shirt, black jeans, and his hair was straight and a little long."

"Sounds like Gideon." Cedric's mouth twisted. "Did you bite any of them?"

Autumn glanced at me wide-eyed. Yeah, since I'd possibly killed one of their own, I could be in big trouble. But I couldn't lie. Once they realized he died of a werewolf bite, I'd be thrown off the estate anyway. And that was the best-case scenario. I had no choice but to be upfront with them.

I straightened my spine, ready to face the consequences. "I got my teeth into him and tasted blood."

Cedric redistributed his weight from one leg to the other as he scanned the vicinity. "Did he bite you back and get the cure?"

Oh, hell. If the other vamps located the guy and found out he drank from Autumn, they'd know she wasn't a werewolf as soon as they noticed he wasn't cured. But I didn't see any way out of that. "No."

"Kayla and Tony, go track him down. Werewolf venom works quickly. He couldn't have gotten far." Cedric's mouth was set in a hard line as he watched them go, and I sensed a rage coming on. I hoped it wouldn't be directed at Autumn or me. We stood zero chance against so many vampires.

"Unless one of the others carried him away," Autumn said as the king's bodyguards sped off.

A woman with red hair skidded to a stop next to the king. "Your Majesty, I heard growling. What's going on?"

Her scent wafted to me and I recognized it from moments ago. Her red hair seemed awfully familiar too. "If you want to get the other three, start with her. She's one of them."

She hissed at me. "He's lying. I was upstairs in my chamber."

Chamber? Who used that word anymore? She must be very old.

"No, Your Majesty, she was one of the four who attacked us," Autumn said, threading her fingers through mine.

"Are you absolutely certain?" Cedric asked. But when both Autumn and I nodded, he asked. "I'm supposed to take your word over my own people?"

I should've known Cedric wouldn't choose us over his own kind. And it wasn't like we could outrun the vamps, especially since we were outnumbered.

Kayla and Tony emerged from the woods with the blond man between them, his arms slung around their necks. His head hung and I wondered if he was conscious. At least I'd already copped to biting him. That knowledge didn't ease the tension building in my limbs or calm the adrenaline roaring through my veins.

The redhead hurried to him, examined his torn shirt, then she gasped at the gaping wound that stretched clear across his abdomen. Black blood oozed from blisters developing over the incision. Yep, I'd gotten the vamp good.

She turned slowly, her fists clenching. "Werewolf bite. If Gideon doesn't get the cure soon, he'll be dead within twenty-four hours. Or sooner with this kind of damage. Your Majesty, I implore you to right this wrong. Demand that the werewolves provide the cure for him."

By now, the redhead had to be wondering why Autumn's blood wasn't working to cure Gideon. But if she voiced her thoughts, everyone would know she'd been with Gideon when his group had attacked us.

Whatever. I did not intend to get on the king's bad side by letting one of his men die. I thrust out my wrist. "Take it."

"Wait." In a fraction of a second, the king was blocking my path. He clutched the hair at the nape of the blond vampire's neck and wrenched his head up. "Tell me who else was here tonight."

Gideon groaned, his eyes rolling around in their sockets.

"Your Majesty, please." The female vampire glared at me. "He doesn't have much time."

King Cedric spun to face her. "Then I suggest you say good-bye."

She gasped audibly, her heart thumping loudly.

"You're choosing a filthy wolf over your own kind?"

"No, Mariah. I'm choosing right over wrong. Gideon and his friends staked my guards." He pointed at the blood on Kayla's shirt, then Tony's. "They disobeyed my orders and attacked innocent *children* under my protection. Your friend will die a slow and agonizing death unless he tells me the names of the others who helped. Then I'll end him mercifully and swiftly."

"But they're the enemy!" Her skin had turned a sickly shade of gray.

"Correction: the werewolves killing our people are our enemy. These two have committed no crimes against our kind. And an enemy wouldn't have offered his blood to heal his attacker." The look in Cedric's eyes became deadly. "As you know, Mariah, the penalty for sedition is death."

"Then it's fortunate I had nothing to do with the attack on your men." She lifted her chin, though her heart hammered loud enough for me to hear.

"The wolves recognized your scent and your timing is convenient. Out of all the nearby vampires, *you* showed up." He waited a beat. "You're lying about your involvement. You'll stand trial. If I let you live that long."

Mariah inhaled quickly. "You can't side with wolves. The vampires will rise up against you."

"And I will triumph, as I have for centuries." He lunged at her, his mouth latching onto her neck. Moments later, she went limp in his arms and he withdrew his fangs. "Kayla, Tony, take them both to the dungeon, then meet me in my suite."

Wow, King Cedric is badass, I told Autumn.

After handing Mariah over to Kayla, Cedric strode toward the mansion, and I tugged on Autumn's hand to follow him. Inside, we sailed through the corridor and up the stairs to the fourth floor. He swept us into his suite, then locked the door. Going straight to his desk, he sat and slumped over.

Autumn and I exchanged glances. We were about to raid the kitchen when he raised a palm. "Please wait. I'd like you both here when Kayla and Tony return." He aimed his chin at the settee against the wall.

We obeyed and sat. From there, we had a view of his profile as his forehead rested in his palms.

After a moment, Autumn said, "Anything we can do to help?"

"I believe so." He didn't offer up anything else, so we resigned ourselves to waiting.

I heard a click, then the door opened and Kayla entered, followed by Tony. Cedric met them at the door. "Sweep for bugs, please," he ordered.

Kayla waved a gadget through the room, spending a little more time with the furniture and anywhere else a bug could be hidden. "All clear."

"Just a reminder that this room is soundproofed, so you can speak freely," Cedric told us, then motioned for Kayla and Tony to make use of the overstuffed chairs around his desk. Once they were seated, he continued. "Thoughts?"

Tony pulled his shoulders back and his voice took on an edge. "I don't appreciate being staked."

Kayla blew black spirals of hair from her eyes. "As much as werewolves disgust me—no offense to our guests—right now, I hate these vampires even more. Being staked always pisses me off, especially by people I believed were my friends. As soon as I find out who else was involved, I'm going to throw them to the wolves. Literally."

"I'll gladly help." Tony leaned toward his king. "You made the correct decision. If you'd taken their side after they disobeyed your orders, they'd probably betray you again and you could lose the throne."

Cedric inclined his head. "My conclusion as well."

"Wait." Autumn scooted forward. "If you were both staked, how can you be alive? Did they miss your heart or something?"

"They didn't miss." Kayla grimaced, rubbing the center of her chest. "A stake through the heart doesn't kill a vampire. Only paralyzes us. If His Majesty hadn't come along, they probably would've finished us off as soon as they'd dealt with you."

Would that be the same way to finish off a werewolf? I doubted Kayla or Tony trusted Autumn or me enough to divulge anything.

"Let me guess," Autumn said, as though reading my mind. "The way to kill a vampire is by cutting off his head?"

Kayla studied her a moment, then looked to Cedric like she was waiting for his consent to answer. After a quick bob of his head, she continued. "Yes. Or dismembering and destroying the body until the blood flow is permanently cut off to the brain. Fire will accomplish that as well if the ashes are scattered."

Hadn't expected that much information. "So, your heart beats and blood flows through your body, same as humans. That's why Gideon's skin was warm when I bit him?" I asked.

"Exactly," Cedric said.

"Ripping out a vampire's heart kills them? Or can the heart regenerate, like werewolves and shifters?" Autumn asked.

Kayla's head swished side to side. "Doesn't kill us. May as well be dead though. Just like you guys, it could take days for us to regenerate enough to do much more than crawl. By then, whoever ripped out the heart would have already finished us off."

I leaned forward, taking her abundance of information as my cue to ask more questions. "I noticed you all walked in the sun earlier today."

"Not all the vampires here can survive the sun," Kayla replied, shifting in her chair to see Autumn and me easier. "Only the stronger vampires. Unless you were created by an ancient, it could take decades to build the strength to withstand the sun enough to stay out longer than a few seconds."

Autumn blinked. "So we're in a mansion full of extra strength vampires who don't want us here? That's comforting."

"Cedric, you'd said earlier that you could drink animal blood and it didn't need to be directly from the vein," I said, seizing the moment while they seemed willing. In this place, I needed all the ammunition I could get. "What about werewolf or shape-shifter blood? Other than using it as a cure, would vampires want to feed from us?"

"We don't usually drink from werewolves unless we've been bitten by one." King Cedric scowled. "Werewolves taste bitter. Shape-shifters go down a little easier, but not our first choice."

Tony snorted. "And witches are delicious."

"Right," I said, grateful that Gideon had been too out of it to mention he'd drank from Autumn or how she'd tasted. If there was any chance the other vamps might detect Autumn, I wanted to know sooner rather than later. "So what's the deal with shape-shifters?"

The vampires exchanged looks, then the king spoke up. "Most of us have little experience with them. Because they're weaker and avoid werewolves, they tend to stay under our radar as well. They usually vanish once any supernatural spots them."

Cedric knew Autumn was a shifter, but the others didn't. I appreciated his effort to cover for her. Cover for us.

"Guess I can't blame them." I glanced at Autumn who seemed relieved.

The king zeroed in on her neck. "Gideon's blood must have splashed on you somehow."

Trying not to appear alarmed, I leaned Autumn's way to examine her neck, but any signs of Gideon feeding on her had already healed. "Yeah, must be blood splatter."

Cedric sent me a pointed look, but he didn't need to spell out how close Autumn had come to being exposed had Gideon or Mariah spilled the beans. Kayla, Tony, and the others wouldn't be any friendlier knowing we were criminals to our own kind. They could end us both with no retribution since we had no value to anyone, no one to mourn us. I mentally crossed my fingers that our secret was still ours and we weren't in extra danger the next few days.

Eventually we'd have to leave the estate and beyond the gates was vampire territory. They hated us. And then there were werewolves. If one of them realized Autumn was a shape-shifter, a werewolf scout may not take the time to bring me to trial. They'd eliminate us both immediately.

As much as I wanted to be there to protect Autumn, staying with her would be the worst idea ever and would only bring us more danger, no matter where we went.

I'd always known our life together wouldn't be possible, extremely difficult at the very least. But I'd let myself live in a fantasy world where we could beat the odds. And maybe we could for a while. Eventually though, they'd catch up to us.

My throat constricted as I forced myself to confront reality: I needed to let Autumn go. But after losing my mom just hours ago, I couldn't lose Autumn too. Not yet. And I couldn't imagine ever being okay with that.

CHAPTER TEN
—— *Autumn* ——

THE INCIDENT WITH Gideon and his gang had been a reality adjustment. Zack and I were in a palace full of dangerous vamps who hadn't bothered to hide their dislike for us and we hadn't been nearly careful enough.

While Zack paced the room, I hovered at Cedric's desk and waited for him to speak up. I'd been grateful for all the tidbits the vampires had shared the last few minutes, but we needed to get on with whatever he was planning. The sooner he got his people under control, the safer Zack and I would be. "So were you faking it earlier when you asked me if you were supposed to take my word over your own people?"

"I was hoping if Mariah believed she had me on her side, she'd offer up information on her accomplices." He rolled his chair back on a long intake of air as his gaze landed on each of us. "All right, the reason I asked you all here..."

I claimed one end of the settee. Zack returned to his spot next to me and gave my knee a comforting squeeze.

"Something bigger is brewing. I can feel it." Cedric

scooted his chair forward to rest his elbows on his desk. "Unless Mariah develops a conscience and decides to share, I won't know who else was involved in tonight's betrayal."

"We could give Gideon the cure, then torture it out of him." Tony gave his king a wicked grin, the chords visible on his neck as he clenched his jaw.

"No cure." Cedric slammed the desk with the side of his fist, his eyes hard. "The others need to know I let Gideon die for his betrayal. That will serve as a warning. As for Mariah, keep her in the dungeon. I'll get to her shortly."

"Your Majesty, if I may..." Kayla rose from the chair across from Cedric and continued when he nodded permission to go on. "I'm inclined to believe the problem is more than a handful of scum trying to get rid of you. A few disgruntled vampires generally don't work up enough momentum or confidence to stake the king's top guards."

"Agreed. They wouldn't show themselves unless they felt the odds were in their favor. There must be many others." Cedric rubbed his temples. "They failed tonight, but I doubt they were set back much since they only lost two men."

"What do you need from us?" Zack asked.

"I hate to ask this of you." Air hissed from Cedric's lungs. "We'll do what we can to discover the traitors in our ranks, but if we haven't solved our little mutiny problem in the next week, I'll need you to stay longer."

"Um." I tilted my head. "How would our being here

help you find them?"

One side of King Cedric's mouth lifted up. "You seem to bring out the worst in my people. I'm banking on them getting more agitated the longer you're here."

"No offense, Your Majesty," Zack said. "But if staying here longer puts Autumn at risk, she should go with her parents. I can stay and help."

My mouth gaped. "No way, Zack. If you're staying, so am I."

"Excellent." King Cedric gave us a grateful smile. "For the remainder of your stay, only my most trusted people will guard you. And Kayla, you'll train our young friends in battle."

Her eyes stretched wide in surprise. "I will?"

"Do you have a problem with that?" He raised one brow.

Kayla studied us a moment, then refocused on the king. "Normally I would. In this case, I'll be more than happy to train them to bite vampires like Gideon." She smirked.

"I'm in," Tony added. He leaned over to knuckle bump Zack.

Though I wished Kayla and Tony hadn't been attacked because they were protecting us, it was nice to know they were no longer hostile toward us.

"One more thing." King Cedric waited a beat. "With Regis out of the country, I need someone else on my side who I fully trust. I'm going to pull Dathan from slumber."

"Do you have to?" Tony slouched in his chair. "He won't be happy about that."

Kayla's gaze darted around the room. "Your Majesty, uh, any chance you can wake him at a time when I'm out of town?"

Cedric suppressed a smile. "No. We need him. He's been in slumber for over seventy-five years, so it's highly unlikely he'll come across anyone here, other than us, who'll know who he is. Which gives us a secret weapon."

Tony waved his hands in an effort to erase what Cedric just said. "Dathan Lacroix tends to draw attention. All anyone has to do is snap a picture and send it to all their vampire friends. It won't take long before someone identifies him and we lose our element of surprise."

Okay, so vampires have a reflection. Good to know.

The king scratched his chin. "He'll stay out of the way and be discreet. His awakening will be between us and we'll all refer to him as... Damon. I believe that's a fairly common vampire name these days."

"What's the big deal about this Dathan Lacroix guy?" I asked. Something about the way they talked about this slumbering vampire set my pulse racing.

"Only the oldest vampire in existence, as far as anyone knows. We rule together. Well, when he can be bothered to rise from his coffin." King Cedric rolled his eyes.

"Rule together as in... you're a couple?" I asked and Zack flinched. Probably not the most delicate question I'd ever asked.

Kayla bit her lip to hide a smile. Tony coughed which sounded more like he was covering up a laugh.

"No," the king snapped. "Not a couple. He's the

true king and I'm the stand-in when he isn't in the mood to do his job. Which is often."

"Sorry," I mumbled, wanting to change the subject as quickly as possible. "So you guys really sleep in coffins?"

"No. That's just a myth we like to joke about." Cedric took a deep breath. "Dathan has been underground since around nineteen-forty and will need to be brought up to speed on modern technology."

Now *that* was something I could do. "I'm qualified to catch him up with computers and Internet stuff."

Kayla stared at me. "Are you sure you want to do that? Because Dathan will probably be a little, uh, grumpy."

I glanced at Zack and grinned. "Nothing I'm not used to."

Zack elbowed me. "I can go over cars with him, point out the new gadgets they didn't have in the forties."

Cedric grimaced. "Dathan barely likes his own kind. Can't imagine him willingly being schooled by a werewolf pup he'll like even less."

"You'll need Tony and me on security," Kayla said. "Unless you want to deal with Dathan yourself, we have no choice."

"And His Majesty can't be let loose in the palace." Tony rubbed his chin. "He'll be confined to this floor, I assume?"

I got the feeling Tony and Kayla were trying to talk the king out of waking Dathan. And since he was the oldest vampire in existence, that had to mean he was the most powerful. If the king's most trusted people didn't want to be around Dathan, how would Zack and

I fare with him?

"At first, yes, he should be kept here. But I see no reason why he can't mingle once he's brought up to speed on modern ways. He'll need a cover, however..." Cedric tapped his fingers as he stared at a wolf-head paperweight on his desk. "We'll say he's a long-time friend. That will justify him staying in the king's suite."

Kayla winced and Tony flinched as Cedric slapped his palms on the desk. "I'll commence the awakening shortly."

Zack and I would be sharing the king's suite with Dathan, no less. Awesome. I shuddered at the kind of damage he could do to werewolves or shifters he didn't like.

† † †

The next morning, Cedric sat at his desk, grimacing at his monitor. "I hate this."

"Trust me." I sat in one of the overstuffed chairs on the other side of his desk, my laptop balancing on my thighs. After clicking the save button on the jpeg, I sent it to my thumb drive, then rose from the chair and leaned over his desk to offer it up. "Your banner."

I rounded Cedric's desk to stand behind him and aimed a pinky at the box that popped up on his screen. "Double click on the file with your name on it. That one."

He clicked on it and his new banner opened. The text announced he was the vampire king, blood dripping off the letters. I'd suggested going with something over the top since humans didn't believe in vampires anyway.

His silence dragged on so long I was beginning to

think he hated it. "You're quite talented, Autumn."

"Thanks." My face split into a grin. "So you're social networking, huh?" I held back a giggle as he switched tabs on the browser to his new Facebook page and then uploaded the banner.

He typed another vague answer into the next field. "My advisors think it will help unite vampires. And they think I should be more accessible to my people."

"Your advisors are Kayla and Tony?" I had a hard time visualizing him on Instagram posting pictures or on Twitter tweeting what he ate for breakfast—which in his case would be blood.

He filled in the next field with an address, which wasn't this mansion. "Yes, as well as my right-hand man, Regis, and the last of my council, Braulio. Once a year, vampire governors from around the world meet and we discuss future strategy, develop new policies. Regardless who my official council members are, I like to stay open to outside suggestions as well."

"Does it matter what any of them think though? I mean, you're the king, yeah? You don't have to do what they say."

"No, I don't. But what's the point in having advisors if you're not going to listen to them?" Cedric swiveled in his chair toward me. "Why don't you smell all shape-shifty? If I didn't know better, I'd think you were human."

I backed up to give him some elbow room, then rested against a short file cabinet. "Yeah, my parents raised me as a vegetarian, because meat brings out our scent."

"Aha." Cedric tilted his head. "And what's your

boyfriend's deal? He seems sad."

My eyes stung and I blinked. "His mom died yesterday."

"I'm sorry." He stood and towered over me, taking in every detail of my face. "You cared for her a great deal."

A tear rolled down my cheek. "She was sick for a long time, so it wasn't a huge surprise."

He brushed the tear off my cheek with his thumb. "You two knew the scouts would come, so you ran?"

"Yeah. We'd been talking about it for months."

He nodded. "I'm glad you both got here safely."

"Thank you for taking us in." I pushed through the sad thoughts of Favianne and offered Cedric a smile. "You're kinda cool."

His eyes twinkled. "You're not awful."

A rap sounded at the door right before Zack burst in and flopped down onto the settee. "Bentley's all good to go. Didn't need anything major, just fluids and a couple of minor parts Tony had delivered."

"Excellent. As for bringing Dathan up to speed on cars, he's still waking up. I imagine he'll be fit for company early evening." Cedric leaned a thigh against the desk. "You two should have some lunch and refuel. You're going to need the energy for training with Kayla the rest of the afternoon."

And for meeting Dathan later. We were going to spend time with an extremely old vampire who didn't like his own people, much less other species. If he decided to get rid of us, could Cedric even protect us against such a powerful vampire?

CHAPTER ELEVEN
——— *Zack* ———

THE GYM WAS all the way down on the first floor. In a normal house, that would be fine. But in this place, it was quite a trek, which left too much opportunity for an ambush. I let out a sigh of relief once we'd passed the threshold, and Kayla locked the door after us.

Mats covered the majority of the glossy hardwood floors. Weapons of all shapes and sizes lined one wall, and another small section held more traditional forms of gym equipment.

Kayla steered us from all that and kept us on the mat with weapons. Mostly *her* with a club while we strained to avoid getting bludgeoned to death. Seriously, with two of us and only one of her, it shouldn't have been so hard. Which made me realize how far Autumn and I had to go before we could take on someone like Kayla.

By the time dinnertime rolled around, my limbs trembled from the hours of avoiding Kayla's swinging club. Sweat dripped down Autumn's neck. She dodged the club and I ducked as it swung around to me.

"Aren't we done yet? I'm getting hungry." I jumped to avoid Kayla's next round of assault.

Kayla advanced again. "If you guys are too wimpy to continue, then say so."

"Oh, I could keep going." I sidestepped when the club came at me again. "I'd just rather not."

She snickered and loosened her grip on the club. Thank God. As I turned to locate Autumn, Kayla's left hook nearly took me down. I blocked it with my right and shoved it away while thrusting a leg out to strike her in the hip. Then her hand came out of nowhere, rotating my foot and forcing me to plunge toward the floor.

Before my head crashed to the mat, new stronger hands clamped around my neck and propelled me upward into the air. "Who sent you, wolf?" A raspy male voice demanded. The man sounded like he hadn't spoken in decades. Had to be Dathan—who detested werewolves.

His chestnut brown hair was overgrown and he wore a full, long beard. His skin was nearly as pale as the white around his ice-blue eyes. He was a couple of inches shorter than me with a lean build, but I wasn't fooled into thinking I had anything on him.

Autumn growled and I rolled my eyes downward to see she'd morphed into a wolf.

Dathan didn't even glance at her. "By the time you bite me, dog, I would've already sucked your friend dry and ripped off his head. And you'd already be too dead to do anything about it."

"Your Majesty, they're here as our guests under

King Cedric's protection." Kayla's voice took on a hint of panic. "He didn't tell you?"

Dathan's grip loosened on my neck, but his brows furrowed. God, I could sense the immense power emanating from him and I quivered inside.

"Then why did you need to defend yourself against him?" he asked.

"This is the training room and we were sparring." Kayla tapped his forearm with her fingertips. "I swear this, Your Majesty. I'd never put our people in danger. You know that."

He released me and I staggered back, rubbing my throat. "Keep these dogs away from me. If any vampire here dies of a werewolf bite, I'll hunt you down," he told me. "Now go."

Kayla gave a nervous laugh. "Your Majesty, King Cedric has asked me to look out for them since there's already been an attempt on their lives. It isn't safe for them to be on their own without an escort."

"We're defending wolves now?" A low rumbling sound began in his throat. "I believe a conversation with Cedric is in order."

"Um." I switched nervously from him to Kayla. "King Cedric will probably tell you that he asked us to bring you up to speed on current technology."

Dathan sneered. "He has me working with a werewolf pup?" His jaw tightened just before I heard raspy hiss, followed by a *whoosh!* and then he was gone.

"That was a close call." Kayla exhaled slowly. "C'mon, let's get you fed."

Forty-five minutes later, we'd ravaged the fourth-floor kitchen. Full and refreshed, we waited while Kayla gained entry into Cedric's suite. From behind his desk, Cedric stood quickly, glancing between us and Dathan who stood by the window. Dathan had cleaned up and shaved, but his hair still hung to his shoulders.

His arms crossed over his chest as he scowled. "It appears I will be required to put up with your canine stench for another week or so." He grimaced at Zack. "Further, according to Cedric, you and the other mongrel volunteered to school me on modern times so that you may earn your keep."

"We need refuge, Your Majesty, from other were-wolves." Autumn took a cautious step forward, letting go of my hand, and my muscles went taut. I didn't like her so close to him. "Considering how outnumbered we are," she said, "you couldn't feel threatened by us."

"As if either of you would ever be of any concern to me." In an instant, Dathan closed the distance and stood in front of Autumn, his blue eyes fierce. Then he zipped over to me, standing so close we almost touched noses. "I could crush you with only two fingers. I warn you that if your true purpose is to spy on us for your werewolf king, I will make it my life's mission to hunt you and your kind until your entire species is no more."

This ancient vampire was the scariest being I had ever known and he didn't seem at all inclined to give us the benefit of the doubt. Sticking around the mansion had become even less attractive than before.

One wrong move and either of us could be dead. I compelled myself to stay still, though my urge to back up nearly overwhelmed me.

I positioned myself next to Autumn again, wrapping my hands around hers to create a united front. "Your Majesty," I said and both kings' heads whipped toward me. "King Cedric," I clarified. "He has no reason to trust us and if I'd lost good men because of werewolves, I wouldn't either."

"Fair enough. But, Dathan, I'm not asking you to trust them." Cedric traveled the several feet to Dathan and slapped a hand on his shoulder. "I'm asking you to trust *me*."

"That I can do, old friend." Dathan waited a beat, making eye contact with me then Autumn, and the tension in the air eased. "I will not harm them unless provoked."

"Excellent. Autumn and Zack will work with you the rest of the evening." Cedric strode to the exit door and swung it open. "I'll be making rounds with Tony if you need anything."

Cedric disappeared and Autumn didn't waste any time at all, like being in a room alone with the most dangerous of all vampires was an everyday thing. "We should learn about computers first. You won't believe what they can do."

She squeaked in excitement, then dashed into our room and emerged seconds later with her laptop.

"I'll be right back." Without waiting for a reply, I slipped out the door in hopes of catching up with Cedric.

Hearing me patter down the corridor, he paused and turned. "Did you forget something?"

"Yeah." I scanned the area for eavesdroppers other than Tony, and leaned in. "I was thinking... in all the centuries you've been around, you must've met more than a few werewolves and shape-shifters."

"Yes, I have." Cedric folded his arms and rocked back on the balls of his feet. "What's on your mind?"

"I was hoping you'd have a way to contact someone from SWAAST. Shape-shifter Werewolf Alliance Against Slavery and Tyranny."

His mouth curved up. "I'm more than a few centuries old. I know about SWAAST." He hesitated and I wondered what was going through his head. I didn't have to wait long. "Their leader is an old friend of mine. In fact, he called me the other day."

I closed my mouth that had dropped open. "You're good friends with a werewolf?"

"It has happened a handful of times. Other than those exceptions, I haven't observed your species to be very likable."

I elongated my spine and lifted my chin. "Which is why I refuse to join them."

King Cedric nodded thoughtfully. "I'll try to reach him."

Exactly what I'd been hoping for. "That would be great. Thanks." Relief flooded through me that I might finally end up where I belonged, but my stomach churned with the knowledge that Autumn wouldn't be with me.

I suspected her parents had been on the run for decades. If they had wanted to join SWAAST, they would've already done it. Which meant Autumn wouldn't be joining me either. And who could blame any of them for not borrowing that kind of trouble?

Because SWAAST members wouldn't conform, the werewolf king considered them the worst of all criminals and they were killed on sight. As Autumn had pointed out weeks ago, associating with anyone from SWAAST was the least safe thing to do.

Her parents would keep running and Autumn would never choose me over them. And she shouldn't, not if she wanted to live.

Autumn and I stuck together the rest of the evening in Cedric's office and educated Dathan on the Internet. We showed him how to use e-mail and by the time we got to smartphones and texting, Dathan sat gaping at Autumn's phone. "These gadgets are swell. Where can I get one?"

"I'm sure Cedric can take care of that for you." Autumn scooted off the settee to grab her laptop from the floor and then Googled modern slang. One side of her mouth twitched. "First thing's first though. Before you speak to anyone else, no one says swell anymore. We should go over the most common slang so you can work it into your everyday vocabulary. You know, blend in with the others."

A half hour later, Dathan sighed. "The world changed greatly while I slept."

"And we've only gotten started." I thought about

all the black and white movies I'd seen with my mom. Everything was so different then. "Women are considered equals in many countries and because of technology, information is instant. Everything's out in the open."

"You'll see when you leave the estate. People wear a lot less clothing, for one thing. Do you need a break?" Autumn eyed Dathan, then turned to me. "Aren't we going to take him for a spin in the Hennessey?"

"It's a two-seater. Unless you have some serious experience driving cars worth millions of dollars, you're staying with Kayla." I leaned over and brushed my lips against her cheek.

"I have to stay in the house, huh?" Autumn grinned mischievously. "Guess things haven't changed as much as we thought."

"Silence!" Dathan shot up from his seat. "You two behave like children. Let's get this over with."

I sent Autumn a look that pleaded for her to get serious. We were already irritating enough to Dathan and we couldn't know what might send him over the edge. I didn't want either of us to lose our head because he didn't appreciate our sense of humor.

Tony met us in the hallway to accompany Dathan and me to the garage. Dathan, his face concealed in a hoodie, muttered throughout our trek as we passed a handful of vampires who sent us curious glances. I had no clue whether Dathan would help protect me or volunteer my neck to them, so I wisely kept my mouth shut and reminded myself not to engage unless I needed to. The more I talked, the more I risked opening myself up to his wrath.

In the enormous garage, I stood next to the Hennessey Venom GT and tried not to drool on the baby-soft leather as Dathan climbed behind the wheel and I slipped into the passenger seat. I spent maybe a minute going over the controls before he fired it up and sped past the mansion gates. His reflexes were excellent and within moments, he was racing through the streets.

Twenty-five minutes later, he backed the sleek car into the garage, smirking as he got out and closed the door.

"Thank you so much for not getting me killed." I wiped the sweat off my brow and squashed the urge to complain further. He'd never had less than one hundred percent control over the vehicle, but riding in a car with a terrifying vampire who was driving over a hundred miles an hour through narrow, bendy roads didn't match my concept of fun. Autumn had dodged a bullet.

As I neared the door to the mansion, my eyes drifted toward the cluster of trees. The urge to run and morph pulsed through me.

"I'll accompany you out this time. Let's get your mate." Dathan dipped his head toward the building.

"I'll call her." *We're on our way up to get you for a run. I'll be ready*, she answered.

Silence clung to us as we ascended the stairs, but Dathan didn't seem to mind. Though I didn't either, I also didn't want to waste an opportunity to drag every scrap of information any of them might give up. Dathan could find me irritating, but I had to try.

"I was wondering... All supernaturals get stronger with age. Is there any point where we can't die?" Since he was the oldest vampire known, maybe it wasn't such a stupid question. I secretly hoped that if Autumn and I survived long enough, we'd be too hard to kill. "Like get beyond death?"

"No, even I can be killed." He slanted his head toward the door to the king's suite. "Just not as easily as you."

"Thanks for the reminder." I marveled at how safe I felt with him, yet so afraid.

CHAPTER TWELVE
─── *Autumn* ───

DATHAN SWORE WE could run anywhere on the hundred acres and he'd never be farther than a heartbeat away. But after what happened last time we'd gone into the woods, Zack and I decided to stick closer to the mansion.

In my wolf form, I ran alongside Zack, our tails whipping against each other. I took in the cool night air and the scent of earth and leaves, wishing it didn't have to end. No other feeling could compare to morphing and reveling at the power of the animal inside. It was as close to perfection as I'd ever known. Well, aside from being with Zack.

He slowed, then pivoted toward me. I halted, not sure what he was up to. *I have to tell you something,* he said.

Uh-oh. *What?*

Cedric promised to contact SWAAST. I'm going to join them.

Wasn't he going to ask me to go with him? My stomach clenched and I could swear my heart stopped. Turning away from him, I struggled to catch my breath.

Your parents will be here in a few days, Zack continued. *You'll be safe with them.*

Though I'd know this was coming, I couldn't let go. *I hoped you'd travel with us for a while.* And then I could put off losing Zack for that much longer.

Zack nudged me with his muzzle. *As if your shape-shifter parents are going to be thrilled about a were-wolf tagging along.*

He made a valid argument. Just because my mom hadn't raged against Zack over the phone didn't mean she'd let him travel with us. But I had no intention of giving up. *We're together. They have no choice but to accept you.*

It could happen. If I thought otherwise, that I would lose Zack no matter what I did, I wouldn't be able to get out of bed each day. I had to keep believing that we would find a way to stay together.

Zack snorted. *How long do you think they've been on the run from my kind?*

Yep, my parents would freak. I whined, lowered my furry belly to the ground, and covered my eyes with a paw.

Sitting on his haunches next to me, he licked my ear, then the side of my face. *The last thing I want to do is leave you.*

Then don't.

"Little wolves, it's time to go." Dathan stood before us, magnificent in his power.

A high-pitched noise reached my ears, but Dathan had already picked up on it. He stood perfectly still and when the shout came, he was ready.

"Werewolf lover!"

Dathan's hand struck out, catching the stake-wielding wrist. "You were attempting to kill me."

The attacker stared in wide-eyed terror as he became aware of the power far beyond his own. And with a stake in his hand, he couldn't deny his intention.

"Who else is with you?" Dathan asked.

"No one," the attacker answered in an unsteady voice.

"Lies," Dathan whispered. "One more chance. Who are your accomplices?" He waited a moment, but the vampire remained silent.

An involuntary shriek escaped me when the vampire's head flew off at the flick of Dathan's wrist. The head landed a yard from me, and I turned away to bury my muzzle in Zack's shoulder.

"Cedric will send someone to clean up the mess. Let's get you two inside."

I wanted to check over my shoulder and see if I recognized the dead vampire. But I wasn't sure if I wanted the gory details. I didn't want to test Dathan's patience either.

As I trotted after Zack, I wondered how many more attempts there would be on our lives if Zack and I stayed together, and how we would survive them all. We couldn't, not on our own.

My parents would never fully embrace Zack and if I followed him into SWAAST—if he even wanted me to—I'd lose my parents. But if I joined SWAAST while keeping my parents in my life, we'd all be marked for death by every werewolf in the world.

I had no clue what to do, but I'd have to make a

choice, and soon.

† † †

Zack set aside a magazine with a shiny red sports car on the cover and raised the bedspread for me to crawl under. "I thought we had a deal. It's hard enough resisting you when you're fully clothed."

"Says the guy wearing no shirt." Dressed in an old tank top and flannel boxer shorts, I slid into bed with Zack. Putting ourselves at risk wasn't a good idea, but if I could lose Zack any day, I intended to use our time well. I snuggled up to him, my arm slung across his midsection, my leg entwined with his.

He bent toward me, his lips seeking out my neck. I ran my fingers through his damp hair, while my other palm explored his bare chest. He shivered. Remembering my limited time with him, I turned away and flopped against my pillow. "Zack..."

He ground his teeth like he knew by the tone of my voice I was about to delve into topics he wanted to ignore. "We can't run away together, Autumn. It's too dangerous. Renzo will probably be looking for us and if he finds me, he'll find you too. No sense in both of us getting killed."

I stared at the ceiling, not wanting him to see how truly disturbing I found the idea of separating from him, maybe never seeing him again. "My parents have been running a long time. If they can survive, why can't we?"

"Your parents aren't mixing species. Much easier for them to stay under the radar. Wouldn't matter if they were willing to take me on, because I can't put their lives at risk that way." He paused a second. "Or yours."

I rolled toward him so we were both lying on our sides facing each other. "I could join SWAAST." I secretly hoped he'd jump on it, beg me to go with him.

"Autumn..." He lifted himself up to rest on one elbow. "I can't ask that of you. You and your parents are screwed just by being shape-shifters. If you joined SWAAST and kept in touch with them, you'd be putting them in more danger. The only way to avoid that is by saying good-bye. Seriously, could you really let them go? Take it from someone who's been there, it's not easy losing your parents."

But losing Zack wouldn't be any easier.

"Don't make this any harder than it has to be," he whispered, gliding his fingertips along my cheek. "It'll just ruin what little time we have left together."

I reached over and switched off the lamp. He didn't need to see me cry. That would make things harder and I already knew his feelings on that. As unshed tears pooled in my eyes, I pressed my lips against his and hoped to figure out a way to keep him without giving up my parents. And I prayed Zack wanted me enough to cooperate.

† † †

The next day, we shadowed Kayla and trained until our muscles turned into noodles. We were wrapping up for the night when a vampire arrived, dressed in baggy jeans and a hoodie shadowing his features. He didn't have to expose his face for me to know it was Dathan.

"Uh, hi, Damon," I said, careful not to use Dathan's real name since anyone could overhear us on the other side of the gym door. "What brings you by?"

He slid the hoodie down to rest on his shoulders and scanned the room. His long hair was gone, shaved about a quarter-inch against his scalp. I imagined getting a simple number-five buzz was probably easier than finding someone in the palace to cut his hair, especially since we were trying to keep his identity a secret.

"His Majesty gave me the thumbs up to mingle so long as I'm discreet." He strolled along the weapons wall, stopping now and again to pick up a dagger. "Thought I'd have a more thorough look at the rest of our new acquisition. When I last saw Cedric, we were in Australia."

"Right then. I'll be in the weapons room." Kayla bowed and disappeared through a door by the weapons wall. I wondered what else could possibly be in that room that wasn't already on the wall.

"His Majesty actually asked to meet me here." Dathan ran his hand along the handle of a sword.

"Why would the king come here?" Unless he wanted a good laugh, he wouldn't want to observe us while we trained.

Dathan shrugged. "Guests arrived. A couple of werewolves, one male and one female."

The new arrivals weren't my parents since my parents were shape-shifters, not werewolves. Surely, Dathan knew the difference. SWAAST? Please, no. I wasn't ready to let Zack go yet. Not that I'd ever be.

"Were we expecting them?" Zack asked with a cock of his head.

"Cedric didn't seem surprised," Dathan replied, continuing his exploration of the spacious gym.

When I glanced away, Zack's arm snaked around me. "This is only a meeting, so I'll know where I'm going after your parents come for you," he said. "I'm not leaving right away."

Still, meeting with the SWAAST guys put Zack one step closer to joining them. And we'd already agreed we wouldn't be on the road together. I buried my face in his shoulder, trying not to think about any of that.

The door opened from the atrium and motes surfed on the sunlight before the door closed again. Zack and I turned to see Cedric, along with a dark-haired man and a girl near our age. My breath caught.

Zack stiffened and released me. "You brought *him* here?" he practically shouted. "He's the reason we're running. To get away from *him*."

Deep gray eyes riveted to Zack's, then slowly approached us.

What the hell was Renzo doing here? I grabbed Zack's hand, willing him not to do anything rash. There had to be some kind of explanation, right? And Cedric had sworn to protect us. If Renzo should attack, we would have help. No need to panic.

I hoped.

Cedric glanced between Renzo and his niece Alura, then back to us. "You asked me to contact SWAAST. So I did."

I nearly fainted from relief. Zack's shoulders unbunched. "You're with SWAAST?" Zack asked Renzo.

Which explained why Renzo had kept insisting he was "on vacation." And why he hadn't eliminated Zack and me when he'd realized I wasn't human and, worse, that I was a shape-shifter fraternizing with a werewolf.

It also explained why he hadn't killed me on the spot as soon as he'd learned that Charles, the werewolf scout who'd been assigned to keep tabs on Zack, was dead and why. It all made sense now. But why hadn't he told us he was on our side?

"And you're running from King Mortimer apparently." Renzo's eyes flared. "Wish I'd known. What now, young Zack? Will you finally trust me or do I need to jump through a few more hoops?"

"Easy, Uncle. We all want the same thing." Alura beamed at us, pretty as ever in a tight-fitting black cat suit. She wore her hair in a long afro and her brown skin glowed. She gathered me into a hug. "I'm so happy to see you two."

I returned her smile. "Yeah, it's nice having a friendly face here." I glanced around the room at Kayla and the two vampire kings. "I mean, not that these guys aren't friendly, but..."

"No one asked you werewolves to come here." Hard lines formed at the corners of Dathan's mouth.

Cedric sent him a chastising look. "The wolves didn't ask the vampires to try to kill them either, but you'd think otherwise by the way our people are behaving. Let's retire to my rooms—which are becoming rather crowded," he muttered the last part. "Kayla, please make sure the guest rooms get freshened up."

Right, because if Renzo and Alura stayed overnight, they'd have to sleep on the fourth floor or risk being murdered.

When both kings, plus Kayla and Tony, had settled into Cedric's office, along with Renzo, Alura, Zack and me, Cedric paced the room. "I was hoping you two would stay a few days," Cedric told the newcomers.

"In a vampire lair?" Renzo laughed as his head wagged from side to side. "No way. This is only their third day here and already several attempts have been made on their lives. Your coven will tolerate *our* presence even less."

Cedric paused mid-stride. "Precisely my point. I'm hoping the traitors in the ranks will become twice as outraged and speed up their plan. Once I've caught who's behind this, everyone goes home. Just give me a few more days. Please."

"If you two can't stay, I'll meet up with you when this is over." Zack cast me a glance.

"You should leave now." Renzo scowled. "What's the hold up?"

I opened my mouth, but Zack beat me to a reply. "Her parents are coming for her, then she's going with them."

Announcing our plan out loud to other people made our inevitable separation so much more real. Nausea swirled in my belly. These next few days were all I had with Zack.

Renzo's gray eyes turned charcoal, making him

seem colder. Which was normal for him, probably because of the zillion fine scars all over his body. But today he gave the impression of being extra worn and tired, like he'd had a lifetime of worry since we'd last seen him. "So you'd rather wait and put yourself in more danger?" he asked.

I had hoped my parents would be delayed until I'd had a chance to map out what I was going to do. I wanted extra time with Zack. But what if delaying him for my own selfish reasons meant risking *his* life. "Zack, I can't let you wait with me if it means you'll be on your own later. You should leave with Renzo and Alura now and be safer."

"Autumn's right." Renzo gave me a disdainful look, his mouth skewing. "No point in pushing your luck here."

Well, lovely. Renzo clearly disliked me every bit as much as he did before.

Zack shot up from his chair, his hands balled as he glared at Renzo. "I want to join your cause, but I'm not leaving her. You can stay or go, I don't care."

Alura laid a hand on Renzo's arm and twisted to face Cedric. "We're staying and we'll help anyway we can, Your Majesty."

Renzo scowled at Zack. "Acting on your emotions won't get you far when you're a fugitive and on the run from the werewolf king."

"Yeah, well, at least I *have* emotions," Zack snapped. "And don't act like you're better than me. I'm not the one who showed up in town and hid who I was and what I wanted."

"Enough, Zack." Cedric aimed the next words at Renzo. "You've been a loyal friend and I can't have any harm coming to you. I regret not thinking this situation through before bringing you here, but there's nothing to be done about it now. I understand you being anxious to leave, but if any of my people follow, you may not survive it. Here you have protection."

"I'll stay," Renzo growled. "But I have an idea I'm going to regret it."

Yeah, in theory Renzo was on our side. But Zack was right about him dropping into our lives without being upfront about his motives. Had he sought out Zack specifically or discovered us by coincidence? My gut told me there was so much more to know about him.

CHAPTER THIRTEEN
—— Zack ——

RENZO AND ALURA accompanied Autumn and me on our nightly run. Dathan went as backup. After a few minutes as a wolf, I morphed back into my human form. With Autumn already at my side, we waited out in the open for the others to catch up. Renzo and Alura emerged from the trees, followed by Dathan.

We'd survived another evening run. If we were alive days from now and made it out of the vampire palace, things wouldn't be easier and I still wouldn't be with Autumn. And Renzo's attitude wasn't helpful. He'd been right though, and I hated him for it. Autumn and I were both safer apart, and I belonged with SWAAST. But out of all the werewolves in existence, why did Renzo have to be the leader?

The smartest thing I could do would be to leave with him and never look back. But I couldn't, not yet. Not without knowing Autumn was safely in her parents' care.

In just a few days, she'd be out of my life forever. Why couldn't I find a way to keep her safe without letting her go? My temples pounded from squashing the need to smash something.

By the time Autumn and I made it back to our room from the woods and we were finally alone, frustration gnawed at me like a chainsaw.

As soon as she closed our bedroom door, I crushed her against my chest. "I'm sorry. I don't know what else to do."

Her cheek pressed against my shoulder as she stroked my back. "About what?"

I framed my fingertips around her face. "The thought of being without you..." My mouth flattened into a straight line. "It's killing me, Autumn."

"Me too," she whispered. "But we could still be together if I joined SWAAST."

I rested my forehead against hers. "Allowing that would be the most selfish thing I could ever do. You're safer with your parents."

"But I'm happier with you." She cupped my cheek, her lashes sweeping up so her gaze could meet mine.

Happier with me... I could feel my heart expanding. When she'd almost died last month and I'd finally admitted to myself I was in love with her, I didn't think I could love her any more. I'd been so wrong. I loved her ten times more now, and I didn't want to imagine my life without her.

But I couldn't say that to Autumn or she'd fight even harder to be with me, and then her chance at living a long and healthy life of freedom would be gone. The deeper she got into me, the more dangerous her life would become.

"Happier with me, huh?" I flashed a mischievous grin. "Imagine how happy you're going to be all night." And then I tossed her onto our bed.

† † †

Right after breakfast the next morning, Cedric ushered us out of the suite and into the gym. With word out that he was not only protecting four were-wolves, but also training some of them for battle, the dissidents could strike at any moment. Autumn and I needed to be ready.

We'd been at it for hours now, me dodging Renzo's attacks and Autumn fending off Alura. It made sense for Alura and Renzo to train with us in order to free up Kayla. She needed to concentrate on her real job—security. But why did I have to get stuck with Renzo?

I sailed across the room and smashed into the wall. Drywall crunched against my shoulder, and I crumpled to the floor. Groaning, I checked to see if I could feel my spine. I wanted all the battle training I could get, but did I really need my ass handed to me over and over? He was supposed to be teaching me to fight, not humiliating me.

I refocused on Autumn and Alura across the room. Autumn was kicking a punching bag, not getting a smackdown. I would've pushed to switch trainers, but I didn't want Autumn to get stuck with Renzo. I'd have to tough it out.

"You're acting on your emotions again." Renzo zoomed to me and held out a hand. Pretending his outstretched hand didn't exist, I scrambled to my feet. "If you had taken a moment, you would've noticed I was anticipating you using your legs," he said.

"Whatever." I turned away from him. "I need a break."

"No, you don't. You've already healed. There's no reason for us to stop."

Fury rose up in me and I rounded on him. "Maybe I don't like getting the snot knocked out of me every five minutes. Ever think of that?"

"Then maybe SWAAST isn't the place for you," he countered. "If you can't take a beating and you're going to give up so easily, maybe you should go with Autumn. Just keep running from every fight. Seems to be what you're good at."

I swung at him and he twisted my arm, pulling me down to my knees.

"This is life and death, Zack. We're only as strong as our weakest member." Renzo released me and shoved me away. "Being impulsive won't help our cause. When you act, think it through and make sure it's right. Lives could be depending on it."

Renzo was on our side—I knew that. But it sure didn't seem that way now. "If you don't want me to join, then say so." I hoped he wouldn't. I *needed* to be a part of SWAAST. Once Autumn left, I'd have no purpose. I didn't think I'd survive without a goal, something to fight for.

Renzo paused, taking a long moment to study me and I prayed he wouldn't send me away. He'd been acting like a douche bag since we'd stepped into the gym, and I couldn't figure out why.

"Why are you so mad at me?" Renzo actually had the balls to look baffled.

Seriously? I was damn near positive that Renzo was hiding something. I just didn't know what and I had little faith he'd cough anything up. I stuck my hands in my pockets, wondering why he had ever been in my neighborhood in the first place. "I could ask the same of you. You're not making things easy and you could leave anytime."

Renzo swiveled away, giving me his profile. He didn't utter a syllable for so long I thought I'd gone too far. "Yes, I'm free to leave and I'm confident I could handle any vampires who may follow. But I need good, honest people to join the cause."

He faced me again, his eyes stormy, giving him the appearance of being more than a little dangerous. "I've lived hundreds of years, Zack, and it wasn't by taking chances. You're young and smart and you could have an amazing future, yet you're throwing it away on a girl who you can never truly be with, someone who will surely endanger you." He tapped my head. "You think with your emotions, but it's going to get you killed."

I could never truly be with Autumn in the normal way. But sex or no sex, I wasn't letting her go yet. Secretly, I hoped she would insist on leaving with me and refuse to take no for an answer. But even as that hope budded in my chest, I knew I was a total jackass for wishing it. "I'm guessing you won't be thrilled if she decides to join SWAAST."

"Maybe you should discourage her." He let out a frustrated growl. "Being with her will make you weaker, and I don't mean that in the physical sense."

"So I should go through life never getting close to anyone? I could do that," I paused, knowing my next words were going to piss him off, "But then I'd end up like you."

His gaze wavered, but he recovered quickly and then his face was once again emotion free. "I think that's enough practice for now," he said softly. "Between what happened with your mom and the vampires after you, it's been a rough few days. You and Autumn should take the evening off. Maybe decompress in front of a movie or something." He gestured toward the exit. "Let's get dinner started."

He wasn't angry like I'd been expecting. He seemed more defeated than anything else. And him not taking the bait gave me no outlet for my rage. Tears burned behind my eyes.

"Hey, Zack?" Renzo brushed my shoulder. "Things are going to get better. I promise."

I doubted that. Renzo acted like less of a jerkface for an entire five seconds though, so I'd take what I could get. At that moment, gratitude flooded through me over the idea of getting some time to chill with Autumn and not having to worry about anything else. He'd been right about the past few days, and I missed my mom like crazy. I couldn't think of anyone who could fill that void better than Autumn.

And once Autumn was gone, I'd have no one.

CHAPTER FOURTEEN
—— *Autumn* ——

DURING OUR BRIEF respite, Zack and I didn't talk about Renzo or joining SWAAST or me going off with my parents. Once I'd checked in with Maya and my mom, Zack and I just snuggled in bed and let ourselves get absorbed into a movie, as Renzo had suggested.

His act of kindness wouldn't be forgotten. Not that I liked him any better, and I sure as hell didn't trust him, but he'd get a pass next time he acted like a douche. Which would probably be soon.

We woke the next morning to the real world and another day of training ahead of us. Bright and early, Dathan escorted us out of the king's suite and down to the first floor. We spotted several vampires as we traveled the staircase and the long corridor. Each sent us suspicious looks ripe with hostility. I'd never been more grateful for Dathan's presence.

"Lock up after I leave," he said as soon as we reached the sanctuary of the gym. "I'll make sure Kayla is monitoring the cameras." He made a circle in the air, apparently meant to include the various cameras in the large room. "If all else fails, you can contact me telepathically. Won't take me long to get here."

"We'll be fine and I'm sure you're needed elsewhere." Renzo didn't even glance at Dathan as he headed toward the weapons wall, and I cringed. Leave it to Renzo to be rude to the one vampire he should never cross.

"As always, no one is holding you captive." Dathan's eyes cut to the exit. "There's the door."

"Thank you for getting us here safely," I said before Renzo could irritate Dathan further. "We appreciate it."

"Uncle Renzo," Alura began, obviously trying to distract him, "shall we get started?"

As Dathan slipped out, I wondered what evils Renzo would unleash upon Zack this time. I suggested we change training partners, but Zack wouldn't hear of it. As it turned out, thankfully, Renzo and Alura worked with both of us at the same time, which kept Zack from being Renzo's bitch and eliminated the need for Zack to avoid him.

Renzo showed us a couple of choke holds and how to wrestle out of them, as well as a few other combat tricks, and later we met in the king's chamber after dinner for a much needed regrouping.

"Your Majesty, our coven is not happy at all," Kayla said from her usual spot in the overstuffed chair in front of Cedric's desk. "It seems everywhere I go, people stop talking. I don't scare easily and I can take care of myself, but knowing there are those among us who could attack at any moment is a bit trying."

That was putting it mildly.

Cedric leaned back in his chair and glanced at Dathan, who was picking lint off his black pants. "Suggestions, Dathan?"

"No." He didn't bother making eye contact with anyone.

Cedric ground his teeth and swiveled in his chair toward Kayla. "Add a few more hidden cameras outside this suite and on the perimeter walls, then send the feed to my computer, as well as yours. I want to make sure we can follow the trail if anything happens."

He refocused on the back of the room. "Tony, I'll need you to be more diligent than ever. No one comes onto the estate without my approval, and no one leaves without my knowledge. Monitor for unusual groupings, people doing things they normally don't, any vampires lingering where they shouldn't be."

"Do what you have to do and don't worry about us." Renzo considered Zack a moment, then switched to me. "If we stay together, we'll manage on our own."

Dathan yawned. "Four of you against twenty-something vampires?"

"We'll bite anyone who comes near us and then run." Renzo's lip curled up. "We've survived that way for centuries under worse odds than this."

Cedric hurled a hard look at Dathan and Renzo from his seat behind the desk. "I'd be more comfortable if you all had backup. Dathan will accompany you anywhere you need to go."

"Can he handle himself?" Renzo asked. By his lack of faith, he couldn't have a clue who Dathan was.

"The attitude is probably, uh, a little misleading." I nodded toward Dathan who was still staring out the window. I wasn't sure if he was even paying attention anymore. "He could probably take out ten vampires by himself."

"Because I'd so rather kill my own kind than filthy werewolves," Dathan muttered, then glanced our way. "No offense."

Renzo's fingers gripped the armrest of his chair. "We'll take our chances alone, but thanks for the offer, Your Majesty."

Knowing we need a change in atmosphere, I stood. "Isn't it time to go out and morph?"

"I believe it is." Kayla rose too and exited, followed by Renzo, Alura.

Just a second, I told Zack and hung back around the doorway, curious to see if Dathan would do something to make himself less of an ass.

Cedric began on a long sigh and gave Dathan a once-over. "Why do you have to be like that? Renzo already doesn't trust you."

"Because it amuses me." Dathan arched one brow. "When you get this old, life can grow boring."

Eyes shrinking with annoyance, Cedric punctuated each syllable. "How can it get boring when you're almost always slumbering?"

Dathan flashed his friend a grin. "I'll watch over the wolves and keep them safe. I promise."

What a jerk, I told Zack, and we bounded out of his suite and into the hallway. Behind me, the door opened and closed, and I could feel Dathan's presence not far behind. Once we'd caught up to Renzo and Alura, Kayla resumed leading us out.

Renzo's arm bumped mine. *You're going to let Zack stay behind to be with you when he could leave with us and be safer?*

I thought you were staying anyway so you don't get ambushed by the vamps. I snuck a peek at him walking alongside me.

He shook his head. *I've survived vamps for centuries. I could get Zack and Alura out of here and leave no trace for vamps to follow. I'm staying here for Zack. I think he'll be a great addition to SWAAST. But if he keeps putting himself in danger for you, he'll be dead and no use to me.*

I had no idea what Renzo was up to, but I wasn't going to let him get away with blaming me for his being here. *Cedric is your friend and you said you'd help him. You don't want to abandon him.*

Renzo scoffed. *Cedric will find his culprit whether I'm here or not. It just might take longer, which is better than losing a perfectly good SWAAST member.*

Was I putting Zack in more danger? I could join SWAAST and the four of us could leave. But my gut told me Renzo didn't want me around. In any case, joining SWAAST wasn't a decision I should make lightly and not a road I should go down without telling my mom and dad first.

Now that I understood why my parents had been overprotective my whole life, I didn't have the urge to push them away and I wasn't ready to leave them yet. But it was either part with them or let Zack go. Either way, I'd lose someone. The urge to cry scorched my eyes.

When we took the last set of stairs, a group of vampires, who I was pretty sure I hadn't met before, hovered at the end of the atrium. They all scowled as we descended.

On the last step, the group of vampires advanced. Kayla held up a palm and they halted. "No one comes near them. King's orders," Kayla said in a firm voice.

"Why are they here?" a brunette asked.

"They are all traitors to their own kind," Kayla said, holding the line between them and us. "We're hoping they can help us uncover the vampire killers."

"If they're traitors to werewolves, they don't have access to any information," a large, sandy-haired male said.

"True, but they know their own kind better than we do." She nudged Zack and motioned me forward. "We'll be on our way."

Another vampire, a tall lean guy not part of that group, appeared in our path. "Only you, Kayla, guarding four werewolves?"

"Make a move," Renzo grumbled, "and you'll be the first one I bite."

"And I'll drink you dry." The vampire sneered.

I wanted to morph into a bear and tear up the vamp just for being such an ass. "It's hard to drink when you have no throat," I hissed at him. "But we welcome you to try."

"All right, let's go." Tony joined us, sending the big vampire a hard look. "You keep your distance."

I could sense Dathan as soon as he was within five feet of us. His energy was unmistakable. "What the little wolf said." He inserted himself between the vampires and the wolves. "I guarantee the only blood-bath happening in those woods will be yours," he told the vampires. "You've been warned."

The big vampire stepped back and the others mimicked his actions. We continued and exited through the back door and kept going until we melted into the small spread of woods.

Before we broke into a run, Renzo bumped my shoulder again. *The longer we're here, the less chance we have of leaving an encounter like that unscathed. Remember that next time you feel selfish and want to give in to your desires.*

Though I ignored Renzo to catch up to Zack, his words shadowed me, clinging to the edges of my mind. I didn't appreciate how Renzo had pointed it out. But I *had* been selfish concerning Zack, so he wasn't totally wrong.

If Zack left with Renzo and Alura, I'd still have a few vampires protecting me. If I copped to being a shape-shifter, and they stopped believing I was a werewolf, maybe they wouldn't want to kill me. My chance of survival was probably pretty good.

We raced into the woods, the four of us morphing as quickly as we could. None of us wanted to delay getting our fur on in case any of the vamps decided to test Dathan.

Even if they opted not to challenge him tonight, there was still tomorrow and the next day.

† † †

As we headed back to the mansion from our long run, Kayla trailed behind, as did Tony and Dathan. I was the first to emerge from the woods, my eyes automatically locating the window to the king's suite where he waited for us. A shadow flitted behind the curtains, and I wondered what Cedric was doing that required such speed.

"We'd better get back to the suite," Kayla said as soon as we morphed back into our human form. "We're too exposed out here."

Once again, I zeroed in on the window above. Something was off; I felt it in the chill crawling up my neck. I rocketed to the side of the building and scaled the wall to the fourth floor. Even slipping a couple times where my feet couldn't get purchase, I made it to the window in mere seconds.

"Autumn!" Zack shouted.

Ignoring him, I peeked through the slit between curtain panels and saw... what looked like Cedric's shoes. But they were pointing up, as if he was lying on the ground. I couldn't think of any reason why he'd be horizontal when people other than us were in his room.

I thrust my elbow against the glass as hard as I could, shattering it. Having shaky footing, my balance wavered and I spilled inside. As I passed over the windowsill, an electrical current raged through me. I jolted and tumbled over a shelf, crashing onto the floor.

I righted myself and morphed into a bear as three vampires lunged for me. Keeping my back to the wall, I flailed, my spastic paws flying wildly. My lack of control from the physical shock worked in my favor, because none of the vamps dared come closer.

In my peripheral vision, Cedric lay on the floor with a dagger protruding from his heart. He wasn't dead, I reminded myself. Only paralyzed. If I could get that dagger out of him, he'd be mobile again and free to help me. Maybe...

Zack climbed through the window, twitching as electric shock exploded through his body, contorting his spine and tossing him to the floor. He morphed into a wolf and wobbled across the room to stand beside me, his fangs bared.

One of the vampires rushed to the window, slammed his palm on a red button that I hadn't noticed before, and a thick slab of metal whooshed down and covered the window. Clever backup security measure.

Unfortunately, I couldn't imagine anyone getting through that barrier to help Zack and me. At least they'd be spared the electric shock. I hoped Kayla, Tony, and Dathan would be bursting through the door instead. Until then, Zack and I had to hold off the vampires a little while longer.

Seeing that they weren't going to get past Zack's teeth and my giant paws anytime soon, the vampires ceased their attack. I was grateful for the chance to regain my balance. *You okay?* I asked Zack.

Getting there, he told me as he snarled at the vamps.

The big vampire we'd encountered earlier held up a hand and sneered. "You won't make it out of here alive. But if you give up now, we'll show mercy and your death will be swift."

When pounding sounded at the door, a smug smile spread across his face. "We scrambled the access panel and that door is reinforced. They won't get by it anytime soon."

But if we had Cedric's help, we wouldn't need anyone to open the door.

I'm going to pull out the stake. Cover me! Zack said. Snarling at the vamps, he slowly moved in front of me, always keeping his teeth toward the enemy. I stuck close to him and roared. Zack was two feet from Cedric when he shouted into my head, *Now!*

I shielded Zack, my paws out and ready to strike when he turned his back on the vampires. I couldn't fight all four who pounced in unison. While still preventing them from getting near Zack, I zeroed in on the big vampire, my jaws opening as he attacked. With his head in my mouth, I bore down as hard as I could and his skull cracked under the pressure.

Another vampire latched onto my shoulder and I swung a heavy paw, knocking him off. His fangs pierced my neck and felt like flames as they ripped my flesh. I batted at the vamp, but he clung to my back, draining me.

Spots danced in front of my eyes and the room dimmed. I wondered where Zack was. Had he been able to remove the stake from Cedric's chest, or had one of the vampires gotten to him first?

Probably didn't matter either way. Zack hadn't been quick enough saving Cedric and, in turn, Cedric wouldn't save me in time. Apparently I could only cheat death so many times.

I kept my jaws clamped shut while my paws swung out at anything nearby. My knees buckled and my head spun as my huge furry body plummeted toward the floor.

CHAPTER FIFTEEN
—— *Zack* ——

IN MY WOLF form, I locked my jaws on the stake. Though Autumn was covering me inches away, I was facing Cedric and couldn't see her. I should've been the one covering her while she removed the stake from Cedric's chest. At least I had the werewolf bite to keep the vamps at a distance.

Autumn couldn't possibly handle all those vamps on her own. But if I didn't save Cedric, Autumn and I would both surely be killed. I had no choice but to leave her on her own. I had to work fast.

C'mon, Cedric, I said as I pulled the stake out. I discarded the piece of wood, careful not to let it roll toward the vampires where they could use it on us.

Cedric groaned and his eyes flickered open. *I won't be much good to you until I feed.*

I thrust out a paw and willed him to drink quickly, while praying Autumn could hold off the vampires until we got to her.

As Cedric's fangs pierced my skin, I glanced over my shoulder just in time to see one of the vamps an instant from sinking his fangs into me. When my jaw snapped, he flipped backward to avoid my teeth. His feet soared through the air, and I stretched forward until my teeth scraped his ankle. He landed, a stream of profanity spewing from his mouth.

Where was Autumn? My pulse hammered when I spotted her bear form on the floor a few feet away. She had her head though, which meant she was alive. That was all that mattered.

The vampire sprang again, diving at me. I couldn't risk Cedric not getting to feed and heal or we were all dead, so I kept my paw still for him while attempting to bite the vamp. He swung around to the other side, and I craned my neck to see him. Oh hell, where was he?

Fangs sunk into my shoulder, sending my flesh ablaze. I tried purging myself of the vamp, but his teeth went deeper and then he tore away a chunk of my flesh. Pain sliced through me and I gritted my teeth. Damn, he'd gotten the cure.

The vamp dove at me again. Cedric disengaged and rammed a fist into the vamp's face, sending him in the opposite direction. The vampire crashed against the desk and I pounced on him, submerging my fangs deep into his abdomen and ripping him open. When his movements became sluggish, I bolted off him in search of another vampire.

There was only one left. Cedric pulled a long knife from his drawer then made a beeline for the intruder who was already fleeing toward the door. I thought about blocking the vamp's exit, but in a flash Cedric pinned him to the floor. He withdrew the knife, then buried the tip of the blade in the vampire's neck. "How many others are there?" Cedric demanded.

The vampire chuckled, liquid gurgling at the back of his mouth. Not my concern at the moment. Autumn had shifted back to her human form, her discarded body lying lifeless, eyes open and staring. I shifted too and knelt beside her.

"She can't be dead," I mumbled as my hands explored her, checking for more serious injuries. Her head was connected, which meant she was alive, right? Panic seized me as I dropped to my knees and brushed the blood-soaked hair off her neck.

"How many are there?" Cedric repeated.

Behind me, the vampire laughed once. "Too many for you to handle."

"They're here in the palace?"

"They're everywhere." He wheezed, his voice weaker with each second that ticked by. "And they'll eventually find another way to get to you."

"Who's they?" When the vamp didn't answer, Cedric shook him and the vamp's head banged against the hardwood floor. "And what do they want?"

"The glory you've been denying them for centuries by keeping us hidden and cowering from the humans." He coughed, followed by a weak laugh. "When you're dead, vampires will take their rightful place in the world."

Cedric grunted in disgust. "Yes, I've read the ancient scrolls, how the vampires nearly killed off their food source. When our species can control their own power, only then will it truly be ours. I ask again, who are they?"

"The very same who will triumph over you," he wheezed.

"Answer me," Cedric demanded, pounding his fist into the vampire—his face, I assumed by the sound of it.

I glanced over my shoulder as the vampire sputtered, red droplets flying through the air. "You may as well kill me now," he said.

"Done." Cedric lowered the sword and I turned toward Autumn, trying to tune out the sound of bone crunching, flesh separating from flesh, and finally, metal scraping against the hardwood floor. Cedric nudged the head away from the body, then stood and repeated the action on the other vampire still writhing near the door. Grabbing the headless body by its feet, he dragged it out of the way. Boots thumped as they fell against the floor.

I heard footsteps muffled across the carpet in the hallway, followed by a click of the deadbolt. An instant later, Kayla, Tony, and Dathan swarmed the room.

"Bastards shorted the panel. Took forever to get through." Kayla's gaze fell to the floor and she hissed. "Autumn okay?"

"Not exactly, but she's alive." Cedric bent down and scooped Autumn into his arms.

"You sure?" I asked, my pulse throbbing at my temples. Autumn and I had learned the hard way that appearing dead didn't necessarily mean actually dead. That knowledge was the only thing staving off full-blown panic and keeping my voice from sounding preadolescent.

"Positive. All supernaturals die to some degree when they would've normally died as a human." He effortlessly hauled Autumn toward our room.

"What does that even mean?" I trailed behind Cedric, barely noticing Renzo and Alura hovering nearby as we cleared the doorway.

Cedric gently deposited Autumn onto our bed. "If our hearts stop beating or we're no longer breathing, we will appear dead on the outside. Inside, our bodies are busy healing, even if there are no outward signs of it." He examined Autumn's neck briefly before straightening and casting me a glance. "Once she's patched up and has a good meal, healing will accelerate."

"How did they get in?" I asked, doing my own scan on Autumn for any other injuries. In addition to the extreme damage to her neck, an ugly wound gaped from her shoulder and blood oozed from her side.

"He was already authorized to access my suite. He must've palmed the panel, then somehow disabled the scanner." Cedric hitched a thumb toward the headless body at the other end of the room. "No one leaves my suite until we've ensured the entire floor is secure. Since I only keep blood bags in my fridge here, real food will have to wait."

I nodded, distracted by Autumn and her open, lifeless eyes. And I couldn't get to any food to help her. "It'll heal faster with stitches, right?" I asked. "Kayla can do that?"

"Kayla can do almost anything." Cedric studied Autumn. "She fought well. I owe her my life—I owe both of you. I can't seem to get myself out of werewolf debt."

I shrugged. "You wouldn't have been attacked if you hadn't taken us in. I'd say we're even."

He leveled me with an intense stare. "The traitors were already here. All you did was help flush them out."

Kayla stood in the doorway, blocking the bright light streaming in from the next room. She held up a metal tray layered with tools and first aid supplies. "Give me some room, huh?"

Cedric whizzed by and I gave Autumn one last glance before stepping out of our room and into his study. I hovered outside our door as Cedric debriefed the rest of the group on how he'd nearly been usurped.

A few minutes later, Kayla flung the door open. "Humpty Dumpty's still sleeping but she's put back together again."

"Thanks." I knuckle-bumped Kayla and, as I squeezed past her, pain shot through my shoulder when I grazed the doorframe. Reminded of the bite on my back, I reached a hand around and my fingertips came back dark red and gooey. Right, the vamp had taken a piece of me. Between that and the energy I'd expended fighting vamps—not to mention Cedric feeding from me—exhaustion weighed on me like cement shoes.

And oh, man, my stomach screamed for food. I craved a big juicy burger with everything on it. I was getting to the point where I'd eat almost anything. Unfortunately, I didn't see food in my future since Cedric had already ordered that no one leaves his suite. Good thing Kayla was gone because even chewing on a limb of a vampire was beginning to seem like a pretty good idea. Their parts grew back, right? They wouldn't miss it for long.

Yeah, I was *that* hungry.

I did my best to ignore my hunger and returned to the side of the bed. Autumn's eyes were closed now and the gray in her skin had been replaced by warmth and a little more color. But she needed fuel to get stronger. So did I.

The door opened, letting in a sliver of light.

"She's still sleeping," I said without turning around. I already knew it was Dathan. Despite my fatigue, I could sense him stronger than anyone else. I muscled through the intense need to nibble on him. My bite wouldn't kill Dathan since he had access to two other werewolves who he could take a nip from for the cure.

"Hungry?" Dathan asked.

"And beyond." I couldn't look at him. He was my natural enemy and my urge to attack had never been stronger. All I had to do was morph into a wolf and I wouldn't care much what I ate. "You shouldn't stay in here with me," I warned in a tight voice.

He rounded the bed anyway and came up behind me.

"Dathan, I should warn you I've never in my life been this hungry. You should leave. Seriously."

He scoffed. "It's illegal to feed from a vampire. If you tried and anyone found out, you wouldn't live through the night."

Another round of hunger ravaged me. "Then maybe you should go."

"But if no one knew...," he said in a voice so low, no one could hear beyond the walls.

My head whipped to Dathan. "What are you saying?" I whispered. "And why would that be on the table? You don't like us, remember?" He was actually volunteering his body parts? A bite or two off his arm?

Yes, I remember, he said, switching to telepathy. *That is a fact I won't soon forget. However, you and your mate showed great courage tonight.* He thrust his wrist at me. *And you saved me from having to play king, a job I loathe.*

Much to my astonishment, Dathan bowed his head and extended his arm farther toward me. When I didn't bite into his wrist, he waved it under my nose.

Do you know what vampire blood does to a wolf or shifter? You must be dying to learn why it's illegal.

Vampire blood? Surprisingly, that sounded tasty. I spun to face him. *Will it make me stronger or will it kill me?*

Stronger is an understatement. The corners of his mouth rose into a half smile. *Drink up. I promise you'll be adequately happy with the result.*

Maybe it was a trick. But it was either that or wait until we could leave the king's suite and access the kitchen. If I got any hungrier, I couldn't vouch for my sanity.

I shimmered into a wolf and nudged his hip with my muzzle. He held out his wrist and I sank my fangs into his flesh. Hot liquid poured into my mouth and my limbs tingled as Dathan's blood spread through my body, flooding my veins and mending my wounds. I understood now why werewolves killed for it. Not so much for the flavor, but for what it invoked—pure bliss, the way I imagined it would feel being jacked up on heroin. Except more intense.

Easy, young wolf. That's enough. He tugged on his wrist.

With great effort, I let go. *Thank you,* I told him silently, then licked my chops and shifted back into my human form. *I can see why it's frowned on. If other werewolves knew...*

"Unfortunately, some do," he muttered. *If it were widely known though, we would be sucked dry and left for dead. The irony of being hunted for our blood is not lost on me, I assure you.* He leaned against the bed, visibly paler than when he'd first walked into the room. *I'll be needing the cure if you don't mind.*

Right. No wonder he was beginning to go gray. He'd allowed me to bite him, fully cognizant he'd be at my mercy until I gave him the cure. But he hated all were-wolves. Didn't he? He could've let me suffer or watched me get so hungry that I attacked Kayla or Tony. Yet he'd been the one to supply me. Ancient blood, no less.

I offered my wrist. When his teeth pierced my skin, the flesh around his fangs prickled. "You're not the jerkface you make yourself out to be."

As if I hadn't said a thing, he waited a few short seconds before pushing my wrist away. *I don't want to take too much or I'll have to refuel you again.*

If someone brought up some food, I wouldn't need your blood, I pointed out.

"Our first priority is handling the dead bodies and cleaning up the pools of blood on the rug. Not to mention the splatter on the walls. We can't risk any of the staff knowing what really happened here tonight. Once we've made sure the entire floor is secure again, we can venture into the kitchen." Dathan dipped his head toward Autumn. "See if you can wake her. We'll need her input." He whirled and strode to the window, and I wondered why he didn't leave.

A light rap sounded at the door. "Come in," I said.

Alura poked her head in and glanced at Dathan.

"They're both alive." Dathan sent her a bored look. "Although your friend here is exceedingly hungry. Autumn will likely be ravenous as well. The sooner we get this floor in order, the sooner we can take advantage of its kitchen."

"Kayla and Tony are on it," Alura said. "And I'm betting Autumn will be waking soon. She was torn up a lot worse last time and she was only out a few hours."

"Last time?" Dathan huffed. "Magnets for trouble. I should throw you off our property as soon as dawn breaks."

Man, he ran hot and cold. Why wouldn't he get out of the room and leave me alone with Autumn?

Alura sent him a frosty look. "Whether we're here or not, you've all been marked as werewolf lovers. Without us here to deter them with our werewolf bites, Cedric will be much easier to get to."

And Dathan could be stuck being king. I hoped he didn't dislike us so much that he'd get rid of us, even after we'd saved Cedric's butt.

As soon as Alura retreated, Dathan resumed staring out the window. I had no idea what was going through his head, but I couldn't worry about that. I leaned over and kissed Autumn's cheek, then the tip of her nose, and finally her mouth.

Her lids fluttered open and she blinked a couple of times, then she struggled to sit up. "What happened to Cedric? Is he okay?"

"He's fine," I assured her, anchoring a hand on her shoulder so she couldn't get up.

"But not that vampire you mutilated." Dathan stood beside me and scowled down at Autumn. Then he offered up a vein. "Drink and be quick about it," he said in a whisper lower than low.

I gave her an encouraging nod. *You won't regret it.*

Dathan allowed her to drink twice as long as he'd let me. Probably because she had more healing to do.

"Enough." He yanked his arm away and faced me. "She's stronger than you. Why do you suppose that is?" The way he said it almost wasn't a question, more like he already knew the answer and was hinting I needed to find out. *Shape-shifters should be weaker than werewolves, as you know.*

"We don't have a clue," I answered. That mystery wasn't my first concern right then and if he planned to tell me, he'd just say it.

Autumn licked her lips and stared at the nearly healed bite marks on his wrist. "Why did you allow that?"

"Despite the fact that your absence is desired by most of my people, including myself, you risked your life to save one of us. You should be rewarded for the loyalty you've shown."

Dathan may have been the scariest supernatural I'd ever met, but he had a solid honor code. I had to give him that, but I wasn't foolish enough to think that would always be in my favor.

He lifted Autumn's chin with an index finger. "You're needed. We'll be waiting for you outside while you take a moment to clean up."

She was needed for what? Had they finally had enough of us, decided that protecting us was too great a risk? Maybe they were ready for the palace to get back to normal, and Dathan intended to follow through with his threat of getting rid of us.

CHAPTER SIXTEEN
—— *Autumn* ——

"GIVE ME A minute," I told Zack. Even though I'd had the best medicine ever and life slowly seeped back into every cell in my body, my energy drained out just as fast.

When you join us in Cedric's office, take care to act weak in front of the others. It won't do to let on I've shared my blood. The fewer who know, the better, Dathan told me, then slipped out the door.

I slumped, covering my face in my hands. I'd almost died. Again. Thankfully, I'd survived, but what if I'd been the one to pull the stake from Cedric, and Zack had held off the vampires? I might not have gotten to him in time. The thought of losing him, of him no longer existing anymore, caused my heart to stutter and fall.

While I appreciate your heroism tonight, as do the vampires I'm sure, what you did was reckless, Renzo silently scolded me from wherever he was. *You risked Zack's life, as well as your own. You'll only ever bring him danger. Set him free now, before he dies trying to protect you.*

"Are you okay?" Zack leaned in to drape an arm around my waist. "Let me help you to the bathroom so you can get rid of the blood."

"I'm fine." I wiggled out of his grasp and staggered to the bathroom. Dathan may have been helpful with the major healing, but my legs still wobbled beneath me. I would've appreciated Zack's support, but doing everything on my own was just what I deserved.

To think I could've prevented the mess if I had urged Zack to leave with Renzo and admitted to everyone in the palace that I was a shape-shifter. With the werewolves gone and the king not harboring the enemy in the palace, his people would've had less reason to rise up against him. Or me.

Instead, I'd been clingy and greedy. Letting Zack go made me want to crawl into a hole, but him dying was a far more horrible thought.

I splashed water over my face and when the water drained back into the sink, it was pink. My own blood... or had it belonged to one of the vampires? A shiver of revulsion danced along my spine.

A part of me hated how thrilled Renzo would be if Zack and I broke up. But I couldn't ignore his logic and continue risking Zack's life, exposing him to danger. First with my ex, then Charles, and now this time because I had acted on impulse. I'd thrown myself into the middle of a vampire war. And once again, Zack had been left to pick up the pieces.

He was always there, putting his life on the line for

me, even if it meant he might be killed too. Because that's the way he was made; he would always step up for a damsel in distress. I loved that about him—his fierce loyalty, how he always acted with honor. And that's how he'd probably go out, loyal to the end. I couldn't let that happen.

Bending over the sink, I stuck a dry, stiff section of my hair under the faucet. The water changed color again. Mine. Had to be my blood.

If I were a cat with nine lives, I'd have six left. But I wasn't a cat; I was a shape-shifter. Since I would always be in danger, my number was coming up. Maybe not tomorrow, maybe not next week. But at the rate we were going, it would be soon. And if Zack were there with me....

Our lives weren't make-believe and I couldn't shut out the real world anymore, no matter how much we wished it didn't exist. Not after tonight. I'd proved with utter certainty that I wasn't impervious to death.

Zack and I had been playing grown-up for months, pretending we could conquer our enemy and beat the odds. But we were only kids just out of high school. Without some advantage, Zack and I would both die like Hannah and Eli. Hunted. And it would be all my fault, because I wasn't able to let him go.

I *would* set him free, though, no matter how much it might rip me apart. Because my happiness wasn't worth risking Zack's life.

He crowded into the bathroom with me, one arm ready to catch me if I stumbled and the other stroking my back. I shrugged him off and leaned my forearms on the edge of the sink, afraid if I faced him he'd see right through me and the story I was about to feed him.

Through my thick wall of hair, I snuck a peek at Zack in the mirror. Knowing I had to push him away, tension burrowed into my chest, but I willed myself to do the unthinkable.

"We're in big trouble, Zack. Vampires are trying to kill us." I aimed a thumb at the bathroom window. "And out there, it's a hundred times worse."

"Like you said, we knew it wouldn't be easy." He hovered inches away.

I straightened and pumped soap into my hand. "I think we're making a mistake."

Zack's arms hung at his sides and his eyelids flickered almost imperceptibly. "What are you saying, Autumn?" he asked too quietly.

I strained to inflate my lungs, unable to get enough oxygen as I stalled, then slowly deflated while I gathered my strength. "I'm only agreeing with what you've been saying all along."

He flinched so slightly, I almost missed it. I grabbed a washcloth, wet it and wiped a spot of blood off my neck. Seconds passed.

"So that's it?" His eyes narrowed to slits, scrutinizing me.

Careful not to show the emotion brewing beneath the surface and threatening to destroy me, I twisted toward him and lifted a careless shoulder. "What else is there?"

Zack nodded, balancing on the sides of his feet. "What happened to fighting for what we believe in, doing what's right?"

I forced out a laugh and rinsed the washcloth under the water. "None of that does us any good if we're dead. I guess having yet another near-death experience has convinced me to face reality."

"So we're breaking up, ahead of schedule even." His eyes were guarded. "After all your big talk, you're giving up?"

I had to remind myself he didn't love me, not truly. If he did, surely he would've told me so at least once over the months we'd dated. His reaction now stemmed from being taken by surprise, that was all.

"Zack..." My voice trailed off and I turned away to stare at the door, hoping someone would barge in and I'd be off the hook from finishing my stupid excuse. "It seems like a lifetime ago we started this." I let my words drop to a whisper. "We're young, with so many things we haven't done. I want to live and do it all."

"That's lame, Autumn. We were never going to stay together anyway, so why call it quits now?" Zack looped an arm around me and hauled me against him. "Look me in the eye and tell me you don't want me."

Knowing my brain would cease all function if I let him touch me for very long, I shoved him away as if he'd burned me.

His eyes hardened, convincing me he was giving up. That didn't take long. "You really don't want to be with me anymore?"

My lips burned to deny it, tell him I loved him more than anything or anyone I'd ever known. "I'm not saying anything you haven't already voiced over and over. Like just the other day."

"You didn't answer my question." His mouth skewed and tightened. "Are you doing this because you don't want me anymore?"

I'd always assumed Zack would get bored of me and would never allow himself to truly love a shapeshifter. In theory, he should've made it easy for me to break it off. He should've walked away and embraced his freedom, thinking he'd dodged a bullet.

Whether he went along with it or not, it didn't matter. His life was at stake, so I needed to sell my story. I carefully coached my face into relaxing. No tears, no emotion whatsoever. I exited the bathroom and shuffled to the bedroom window, same as Dathan had done so often, which made him seem so detached. I gazed out into the night sky, seeing nothing. Except Zack's reflection in the window as he closed the distance to stand beside me.

"I guess I'm having a hard time getting past the drawbacks to see the advantages." I glanced over my shoulder at Zack and shrugged. "We had a great ride, but now it's time to grow up and move on."

He folded his arms over his chest, his chin angled down as he glared at me. "If that's the way you feel, then there's no point in staying together the next few days."

That was the Zack I'd expected. Resilient. Strong. He'd be fine without me. "My thoughts exactly."

I turned back toward the window, looking past his reflection and focused on a swaying branch. I imagined myself there, sitting in the morning sun with a breeze grazing my cheek. Anywhere but here and now. I sighed for effect and zipped to the closet to grab a scarf. I wrapped it around my neck so the others wouldn't see the lack of scarring and suspect I'd had vampire blood.

"No problem." He raised a palm and growled so low, I almost missed it. "So much for values, huh, Autumn? I guess it didn't take you long to slip back into your old self." He advanced a step. "You know, when we're done here, you could go to college, join a sorority, and continue on up the social ladder." His tone took on a hard edge. "With your people skills, I have faith in you."

He slammed the door shut and the next moment, I stood alone, my fingers trembling. I collapsed onto the bed, balling up in the fetal position. Squeezing my eyes shut, I jammed a knuckle against my mouth to suppress a sob.

I couldn't lose it now. The others were expecting me to join them.

Breathe in. Breathe out. I unfurled my legs and spine, then rolled off the bed and planted my feet on the floor.

I'd get through this and Zack would be fine. He'd get over me. Whoever he ended up with, he would *live* and that's what mattered. I, on the other hand, couldn't envision myself surviving long after we left Cedric's refuge. It wasn't that I *wanted* to die. More like, I wasn't sure I wanted to live. Some things weren't worth fighting for. Not without Zack. I'd make sure he survived though. And I'd make sure he forgot I ever existed.

A teardrop made its way down my cheek, leaving a wet trail. I could smell the mixture of salt and water. Air fluttered past the wet path and cooled my hot skin. The tear wasn't for me, but for Zack. As reluctant as he was to voice his feelings for me these past months, I knew he cared deeply. He'd come through too many times for me to doubt that. But that wasn't the same as being in love.

The door opened and I immediately smelled metal and musk. Cedric. I wiped my eyes, trying to keep my movements fluid so he wouldn't suspect I was hiding something.

"There you are. Came in to see what's taking you so long." After a moment, Cedric tipped his head. "Something wrong?"

I faced him and roused a smile. "No. Just whining to myself how hard life can be," I muttered. That was an understatement. And it was probably going to get a whole lot harder.

CHAPTER SEVENTEEN

——— Zack ———

AUTUMN HAD BARELY looked at me since she'd thrown the grenade an hour ago, when she'd reached into my chest and yanked out my heart. We were at war with vampires and she'd broken up with me when we needed each other most. I was drowning in my own blood and, rather than fight for her, I let her go. I wasn't sure whether to be angrier with her or myself.

Not like I had a choice; I had to give Autumn what she wanted. As much as I believed she'd done the right thing, I also hated being dumped. I hated how she'd minimized everything we'd shared. I hated that she'd discarded my feelings, how she'd cringed when I'd tried to hold her. Mostly, I hated not being able to tell her how much I loved her, that the idea of being without her caused my lungs to ache and my heart to crash against my ribs so hard I thought they'd splinter.

In all the weeks we'd spent together, not once had she wavered. Not once had she seemed bored or less affectionate or treated me differently. After all her persistence to finally get me where she wanted me, now it was all a mistake? I wasn't buying it. But I couldn't allow the situation to distract me. Our lives were at stake. Whether she loved me or not, I loved *her*. No way would I allow her get hurt without putting up a fight.

After we'd raided the kitchen on Cedric's floor, he and Dathan requested that Kayla call a mandatory meeting for all vampires on the estate. Dathan and Tony had accompanied her for protection. Autumn and I, along with Renzo and Alura, stayed behind and crowded around Cedric's monitor where we had a digital view of the entire gym. A steady chatter streamed from Cedric's speaker as vampires milled about, waiting to see what Kayla had to say.

Through the monitors, the training room hushed as Kayla hopped up onto the table and bowed her head.

"A tragic thing has happened and our beloved King Cedric is dead. Decapitated in his own chamber after being staked through the heart." The vampires gasped, but she didn't give them time to mourn. "Surveillance cameras in the area were taken out, so the assailants are unknown to us. I beg that anyone with information please speak with me before you return to your duties."

Cedric hit a button and the monitor split in two, one side zoomed in on Kayla, the other panned the audience.

"Since no one has entered or left the estate these past few hours, the murderer must be among us. Therefore, the estate will be under lockdown until Regis arrives and King Dathan can be located and awakened from slumber."

"How long will we be under lockdown?" the vampire who I recognized as Gustov asked.

"Regis is in South Africa dealing with one of our diamond suppliers. We're working on getting him a flight, but..." she rubbed her temples and I admired her acting skills, "since it takes over twenty hours to get here by plane, it could be a couple of days to arrange a flight and travel."

"So we're trapped here, fighting over blood bags?" A shorter vampire with inky hair grunted.

She shot him a withering stare. "If that's how you want to play it, fine. But you and I both know we keep an emergency blood supply on every floor."

The vampire snorted. "Will we get compensated for our troubles?"

"For staying in a palace you probably hadn't planned on leaving anyway?" Kayla hissed and bared her fangs. "Do you think your king will be compensated for his death? And those of us who will mourn him, will we be compensated?"

"The wolves killed him," a man called out. "They're the ones who should be under lockdown."

"No," Kayla hissed back. "I was with them in the woods when the king was attacked. We left His Majesty alive and when we returned to his suite, we found him dead. Those of you who know me well can't believe that I would protect guilty werewolves."

"We don't question your loyalty, only your naïveté," a woman said. "I've never met a wolf who could be trusted."

"That may be," Kayla said, her jaw flexing. "But these particular wolves are innocent in the king's death and they will remain here under our protection, as he wished. I beg that you all remember our king as the strong ruler he was and stay true to his laws and wishes. That is all."

Murmurs rustled throughout the gym as the vampires disbanded, many of them eyeing Dathan as they filed out of the gym. But he kept the hoodie shadowing his face. Which probably made the others even more curious.

A tall, lean vampire stood below the table and tilted his chin up to see Kayla. "Milady, this is a sad time for all and you have my condolences. Please tell me how I can be of service."

She smiled, but the light didn't reach the rest of her face. "Thank you so much, Renault. Your support means the world to the rest of us. I won't hesitate to call on you should I need anything." She kept him in her line of vision as he bowed and made his way out of the room.

Next to me, Cedric swiveled in his chair toward us. "With me dead, Kayla remains to hold the reins, which makes the throne appear at its most vulnerable. No better time for them to strike."

A 'v' formed between Autumn's brows. "The traitors are going to wonder why their four men haven't checked in after assassinating the king."

"They'll suspect a trap," Cedric agreed. "But they

also know Regis is on his way, and the true king is being located and eventually awakened. With Regis and I against them, their chance of success is greatly decreased. Any actions they take must happen in the next day or so, or they may have to wait years before they have another opportunity to gain control."

"Who's Regis again?" I asked, sneaking a glance at Autumn who still hadn't looked at me even once since she'd emerged from our room.

"Our right-hand man," Cedric answered. "He's young, but he's brilliant with security, technology and warfare."

When Kayla entered the room, accompanied by Tony and Dathan, everyone's attention riveted to Cedric's desk where a cell phone vibrated. He picked it up and checked out the screen. "Braulio just arrived with Regis," Cedric announced. "He will access the estate normally, but Regis is taking... the other way."

Which brought our group total to one shapeshifter, three werewolves, and six vampires.

"The other way?" Autumn asked. "Secret tunnel?"

"Something like that," Cedric answered, tapping his fingers on the glossy surface of his desk.

"How did you keep the builders quiet about the tunnels?" I asked.

"The areas I wanted confidential, I did myself." He studied the screen.

Kayla inserted herself between Cedric and his monitor, tapped a few keys, and rows of security feeds showed up. "Ah, there's Braulio at the gate, working his charm on Guinevere who already knows to grant him entry."

She pointed to another camera feed where a black-clad man was stooped over and traveling through a narrow passageway. A tunnel, I assumed. I understood now why Cedric had built the place himself instead of buying something already done.

A few minutes later, the wall on the other side of Cedric's desk thumped. Cedric rose, ran his hand over the smooth cream-colored surface, then pushed and the door creaked open. The black-clad man ducked to clear the doorway. He had sandy-blond hair and towered over everyone.

"Regis, good to have you back." Cedric nodded.

"Your Majesty." Regis bowed then cast a glance around the room before greeting the outsiders as warmly as he greeted his own kind. Autumn smiled back at him, just as friendly. My stomach gave a sickening lurch, and I hoped neither of the newcomers was single. Autumn would eventually find someone new, but damned if I would let her hook up with anyone while I was around to witness it.

Cedric had barely finished introductions when Braulio arrived. He was a little shorter than Regis with dark wavy hair, olive skin, and dimples. Jesus, couldn't any of these vampires be ugly? I doubted Autumn would venture outside her species again after what we'd been through. Then again, I was beginning to wonder how well I knew her.

The new arrivals settled into their chairs and Cedric spent the next few minutes catching them up on recent events. When Cedric finished recounting how he'd nearly been killed, Braulio's gaze scanned the various faces in the room, finally resting on his king. "Does anyone have a plan?" he asked.

"Possibly, but I loathe discussing strategy on an empty belly." Still standing, Cedric flattened his palms against the top of his desk. "Tony, have some blood bags brought in, maybe another snack for the werewolves. Kayla, we'll need to make a trip to the training room to load up on weapons, but I don't want you two going anywhere without backup. Regis and I must stay out of sight, so take Dathan with you, got it? And if anyone attacks, we'll see it through the feed. Won't take us long to get there."

"Yes, sir." Kayla wagged a finger between Autumn and me. "You two, keep practicing. They could attack at any moment and you need as much training as you can possibly squeeze in."

We'd be back to training tomorrow, assuming we weren't ambushed tonight. I wasn't looking forward to leaving the safety of the king's chamber to travel to the gym where anything could happen along the way.

CHAPTER EIGHTEEN

——— Autumn ———

THE WEREWOLVES STILL needed a safe haven, but so did Dathan and the new arrivals. Tony and Kayla had to be kept safe too, not only because they'd stood up for the werewolves, but because they were the immediate barrier between the enemy and the throne.

Cedric had the entire floor with plenty of rooms to accommodate everyone. But the security wasn't as strong outside his suite, and only his rooms were soundproofed. The limited space available forced Zack and me to continue sleeping in the same bed together.

With Kayla taking up the small sofa in our room, I wasn't at all tempted to snuggle with Zack. That went double considering Renzo had stretched out over thick layers of blankets on the floor.

The next morning, as we prepared for our day, Zack acted like he didn't see me as he rolled off the bed and went straight to the bathroom to shower. After breakfast in the king's chambers, the vampires escorted us to the training room without incident, and I breathed a sigh of relief. We'd probably be safe there for the next few hours with the doors locked. I hoped.

I sparred with Alura, as usual, and Zack trained with Renzo. But sometimes Renzo and Alura teamed up to demonstrate a move, which put me practicing with Zack. Because I got lightheaded every time he came near me, I'd begun stepping away from him whenever possible, in hopes of avoiding his musky scent. Stupid hormones. Stupid me for wanting him so much.

During moments between sparring, I'd even twist around so I couldn't look at him. So long as I couldn't see him and his scent wasn't invading my senses, I could be around him without dropping to my knees and pleading with him to take me back.

After lunch, Dathan checked in and stayed for a few minutes. I hovered by the door in the weapons room, waiting for him and Zack to finish debating which was a cooler weapon, the cyclone tri-blade or the sword. I'd already grabbed a couple of daggers that would morph with me, hid one in my boot and the other in my pocket. I wouldn't be able to hold a weapon in my paws once I morphed into a bear, but I wanted to be on the safe side.

"The tri-blade is only useful if you can use it properly." Dathan nodded at the three blades shaped into a disc. "Swords require training too, but they're more straightforward."

Zack snorted. "Hey, I'm no expert, but if I was gonna get trained in something that wasn't an assault rifle, it would be a bow and arrow. Using blades requires you to be close to your opponent. I'm thinking distance between vampires and me is a pretty good idea, thank you very much."

Dathan snickered and they switched to the bows and arrows. Being total boys, they could be there a while.

"Step away from the toys, you two." I rolled my eyes. "We have training to do."

"Party pooper." Zack grinned and snagged me around the waist then leaned into me like he was about to tag my nose with a kiss. Then his eyes stretched wide, his face fell, and he released me. "Right. We don't have all day."

My stomach dropped like a headless vampire. Zack had fallen into our old routine, reminding me why I loved him, which made me miss him even more. I wanted to tell him I'd made a mistake, that he was my whole world and I'd been an idiot to throw away these last few precious days with him. But that would make our bond stronger and our future breakup even harder.

Dathan took off and for the next few hours we trained. When Zack slid across the slick wood floor and slammed into a wall, Alura stopped her assault on me. We both turned as Zack leapt to his feet and charged his opponent.

Renzo redirected Zack's momentum and sent him flying again. "You're acting on your emotions."

Favoring his left leg, Zack pulled away from the wall, his face flushed. "Maybe I'm tired of getting my ass beat over and over."

"Didn't we have this exact conversation a few days

ago?" Renzo asked.

"Yes." Zack's jaws clenched. "But you're still being a dick."

"The good news? You won't be tired of me when you're dead," Renzo said, leaning casually away. "Which you will be soon at this rate."

I stepped toward them in an effort to lighten things up, but Alura snatched me back by my elbow. "They need to work this out on their own," she whispered.

Alura was right. Zack had to work it out without my help or support. I wasn't his girlfriend. But if I hadn't deserted him, maybe things with Renzo would've gone a little smoother. I felt like a horrible person doing that to him just days after his mom died. Worst girlfriend ever. Correction: worst ex-girl-friend ever.

"What's your problem, Renzo?" Zack clenched and unclenched his fists. I'd never seen him that furious. "How can I learn from you when you're spending most of the time pounding on me? And when the fight comes down, I'll be too beat up to do anything."

"You'll heal soon enough," Renzo growled. "Damn it, Zack, I'm trying to teach you how to survive."

"Then teach me and stop trying to get inside my head. You're not my father and you're not my friend."

Ouch.

Renzo drew in a lungful of air and turned from Zack like he was getting his temper under control.

Alura left me and sprinted to her uncle. "Maybe you two should take a break from each other. I can work with Zack."

And leave me to work with Renzo? I winced at the thought. But at least it would give Zack a much-needed break.

"No." Renzo held up a hand to stop her. She took a step back and he waited a beat before facing Zack again. "I apologize."

"What?" Zack's mouth dropped open.

"I'm sorry. Obviously, my teaching method isn't working for you." He pinched the bridge of his nose and hesitated a moment. "See, the thing is... I can't allow anything to happen to you. And from my observation, your biggest mistake—other than your lack of combat skills—is that you let your emotions control you. Any action driven by negative emotions is often the wrong one."

Zack folded his arms over his chest. "I'm not a machine, Renzo. If I'm under attack and my life is at stake, I'm probably gonna be scared which can't help but affect my decisions."

"Then let's practice ignoring your fear and concentrating on kicking some ass."

"So you're not going to beat the crap out of me anymore?" Zack asked, one brow cocked.

Renzo laughed. "Of course I am. But I'll try to be less of a jerk about it." He reached his hand out. "Deal?"

Zack stared at Renzo's hand, then slowly reached out and grasped it.

Emotion flickered over Renzo's face, but it was gone too quickly for me to read. What was up with that guy?

Zack's opinion of him seemed to matter an awful lot. And something, maybe fear, was making him push too hard. But why?

"You ready?" Alura asked, snapping her fingers in front of me.

I refocused on Alura. "To get stomped on again? Absolutely. This is the most fun I've had in ages," I said wryly.

She chuckled and stepped behind a punching bag, gripping both sides. "Let's switch things up a bit. Take your best shot."

I drew back my arm and Alura released the bag as I thrust a fist at it.

"Whoa. That's horrifically bad form." Renzo must have been eavesdropping because he was already beside me by the time I caught his scent. A moment later, Zack joined him.

"Gee, thanks. Feel free to give me some pointers," I said, hoping to provide a respite for Zack from Renzo's abuse.

"For starters, you need to improve your stance, Rossi," Renzo told me. He aimed an index finger at his feet that were shoulder-width apart. "Zack, pay attention to this. You two may as well work on it at the same time." He flattened his lips together, clearly amused. "Then you can get mad at *her* for hitting you."

"I'm sure I can find another reason to be mad at you. And her," Zack mumbled.

Renzo's smile faded. He zeroed in on Zack as if trying to read his mind. Alura was staring at the men just as intently as I was.

"Care to share what else I'm doing wrong?" Renzo asked.

"C'mon." Zack tossed his head back. "You've been hiding something since the first moment we met you. I want to know what it is."

"Fair enough." Renzo straightened, his chin tilted up. "When you're ready, I'll tell you."

Zack hissed. "That's the best you can do? 'Cause we could die today."

"Then we die and it doesn't matter anyway." He took the sparring stance, feet apart, loose fists close to his face. "Punch me."

Without hesitation, Zack's fist shot out. Renzo's arm struck a fraction of a second later, blocking Zack and punching him in the nose. Zack staggered back and glared as he wiped blood from his upper lip.

Renzo slanted his head. "You're exceptionally strong for a newbie, but you have no idea what to do with all that power."

Zack didn't comment and Renzo gave him a strange look. Rather than betray Dathan's trust and explain why Zack was unusually strong, I kept my mouth shut.

"There are many ways to punch." Renzo's mouth curved up on one side. "My favorite is to thrust an arm out, turning my wrist as I go, but also bringing up the elbow." Renzo demonstrated in slow motion. "See how the elbow is up? My arm is not only in a position to do damage, but it's also shielding my face. If you were to return fire, you wouldn't reach your target."

Zack's fist flew again and clocked Renzo in the chin. "Like that?"

"Yeah." Renzo rubbed his jaw, pride gleaming in his eyes. "Like that."

CHAPTER NINETEEN
—— *Zack* ——

GETTING A PUNCH in on Renzo had felt good. Damn good. After all the weeks of stressing over why he'd been hanging around—only to learn he was the leader of SWAAST—his reluctance to cough up the last of his secrets irritated the hell out of me.

If he'd been upfront about who he was, Autumn and I would've been saved so much anxiety. And we wouldn't have had to run away and end up in a palace with vampires out for our blood. And maybe Autumn wouldn't have broken up with me.

And yet I felt like an ass. Back home, Renzo hadn't known my true intentions. In fact, I'd lied and told him I planned on joining the king and becoming part of a pack. It was the only story I'd been able to offer since I'd assumed he was a scout and loyal to werewolves. Taking me at my word, Renzo would've had to be crazy to tell me who he was.

And if Autumn's feelings for me had changed because of my actions, that wasn't Renzo's fault.

"Are you going to try to hit me again or not?" Renzo

asked. When I hesitated, he moved from behind the punching bag. "Something wrong?"

I relaxed, bringing down my fists. "I should apologize for being a dick to you. You couldn't have told us who you were, not if you thought I was loyal to King Mortimer."

Renzo sagged against the punching back, rubbing his neck. "No apology necessary."

I raised my arms, shielding my face with my fists, ready in case Renzo wanted to go back to sparring. His eyes bounced off Autumn and he softened his voice. "Speaking of loyalties, what's your plan with her?"

The memory of losing her ravaged me, making my head ache, and I wished Renzo would shut up about Autumn. "I try not to think about it."

"Think about what? That she'll slow you down? That mixing species is a capital offense and you'll probably live longer without her?"

My shoulders stiffened. Right when I was warming up to him, he pulled something else. "I didn't ask you to like her."

"My antipathy toward her has nothing to do with anything. Zack, being with her could get you killed. For that reason alone, I can't allow myself to form any attachment to her. Neither can you."

Too late, I said silently so Autumn wouldn't hear. Across the room, she landed a punch and Alura stumbled away. Yeah, my baby killed it. *Without her, I think... I'd probably die slowly from the inside out.*

Renzo rested his fists on his hips. *And yet, dying slowly that way, you'd still live longer than if you stayed with her.*

"Or not." Just because she'd broken up with me didn't mean it would be permanent. We had always planned to split up in the future. But being without her made me realize I'd never willingly give her up. Ever. And if she gave me any kind of hint at all that she wanted me, I fully intended to win her back. *Maybe it's more a matter of strength in numbers. Maybe we're stronger together than apart.*

Without hope that we'd be together again, what reason did I have to fight for my life? I had thought—hoped—I could let her go, but I knew better now. The fact that something didn't quite ring true with her breakup speech gave me real hope. And if she'd lied about not wanting me, I had time to get the truth out of her.

Even if mixing species had no effect on either party, Renzo said, *King Mortimer will still look for you. Eventually, he'll learn about you being with a shape-shifter and hunt you both ten times harder.*

"Yeah." I glanced at Autumn again who was practicing kicks. *She's worth the risk.*

Renzo hung his head and rubbed his temples. *I know what it's like to love someone of a different species. But if you can resist, everyone's better off.*

That got my attention. *You fell in love with a shape-shifter?*

"No." His eyes took on a faraway look as his mouth curved down.

"Human, huh? They don't count though, because you can change them. Then you're no longer different species." Unless they're too sick, like my mother.

"True." Renzo blinked then his gaze wavered.

"What happened to her, the woman you loved?" I asked.

He turned toward the door as it swung open. "Lunchtime."

Yeah, as if he was going to open up to me about his love life. Whatever. We shoved all the weapons to the other end of the long table and the girls set up the trays of food.

The four of us devoured our BBQ ribs in silence—except Autumn who stuck with mashed potatoes and corn on the cob. After a few minutes, Alura dabbed her mouth with a napkin as she scanned our faces. "Autumn is surprisingly strong."

Renzo chewed as he studied me. "Interesting. So is Zack."

"Maybe my parents are fairly old," Autumn suggested.

"Doubtful." Renzo scoffed. "Shape-shifters aren't allowed to live long for that reason. Werewolves can't have the lesser species running around getting stronger and stronger, can they?" he asked dryly. "They are, however, kind enough to grant their slaves a hundred years or so of servitude before they kill them."

I tapped my chin, contemplating that new bit of information. "Maybe her parents escaped. Either way, *my* dad could've been an ancient."

"He wasn't." Renzo's tone was so decisive he had to know firsthand. "In any case, even an ancient requires sufficient time to heal. Autumn nearly lost her head and a half hour later, she was almost good as new. No one heals that fast. Trust me, I have experience in that area."

How the hell did Renzo know anything about my dad? I stared at him, waiting to see if he was going to add anything else. Autumn had stopped chewing, shifting her attention between Renzo and me. Apparently, I wasn't the only one who'd interpreted his comment as odd.

"Care to elaborate?" I asked.

Without making eye contact with me, he dragged his tray closer. "About what?"

"You being so certain my dad wasn't an ancient. You don't think I'm going to leave it at that, do you?" When Renzo merely shrugged, I forged on. "You knew him."

"Sort of." Renzo continued eating without glancing up.

I gritted my teeth, wishing I didn't have to pull the information out of him. "Renzo, my dad died when I was just a little kid. I don't have any pictures of him and don't remember what he looked like and that's all you're going to give me?"

Renzo dropped the last bare rib and pushed his plate away. "I'll tell you as much as I can."

"Were you two friends?" I asked.

"I suppose. But Lucio didn't let many people in. He loved your mother fiercely though."

Yeah, I knew that much. I leaned forward, hoping to keep Renzo's attention. With my mom gone, Renzo was my only source of info on my dad.

"I used to think he was alive. My mom didn't tell

me much about how he died, but we both know what it takes to kill a werewolf." Thinking of my mom made my heart weigh heavy in my chest and tears threatened to turn me into a crybaby. "But if he were alive, he would've never let my mom die. He'd find a way."

Renzo's eye twitched. "Maybe. If there was any good left in him, he probably would've found a way to save her."

What was that supposed to mean? That my dad had let her die because he was a sucky person? Okay, now wasn't the time to get all defensive, not if I wanted Renzo to talk. "He left a letter for me, along with some other things. He seemed conflicted, like he wasn't sure whether he was the good guy or the bad guy. But my gut tells me he was okay."

"I guess there were times you could call him the bad guy. I think he *wanted* to be good." Renzo rubbed his chin a moment, then suddenly stood. "We should get back to work. If things go down the way I think they will, we need to be prepared for an attack tonight."

Right, of course. Being locked in the gym these past few hours had given me the illusion of safety, and I'd forgotten that the traitors would want to take control while the throne appeared vulnerable, before Dathan and Regis arrived and made it more difficult. Possibly hours from now.

CHAPTER TWENTY
——— *Autumn* ———

NO WAY WOULD I be ready for battle so soon. The traitorous vampires had decades, even centuries, of combat experience. I'd had a few *days* of training. I could only hope that Cedric and Dathan were wrong and the vamps wouldn't strike so soon. Maybe there were no other traitors. Maybe they'd all been killed in Cedric's suite.

Yeah, sure.

"How about we try some new toys?" Alura rose from the chair and headed for the weapons room. The rest of us followed. Looking at shiny knives might take my mind off the imminent battle. "We could work on fencing," she said, examining the row of blades.

Renzo selected a sword in no time. "Make sure you choose one with a comfortable grip and appropriate weight. I'll be outside."

Alura tested several swords, slicing them through the air before settling on a long, narrow one then she vanished from the room.

I concentrated on finding my own weapon. Facing

the wall next to Zack, I wanted to stroke his back or run my fingers through his hair. I kept my hands busy checking out one sword, then another, waving them side to side to get a feel for their balance. "Maybe we should give Renzo a break. Regardless of any secrets he's keeping, he's still on our side. For all we know, he has a good reason for not telling us whatever it is."

"You're probably right." Zack skimmed his knuckles against my cheek, then yanked his hand away and growled. "This is stupid, Autumn. I'm having a hard time believing your feelings changed so drastically from one second to the next."

"Stupid or not, it's the truth." I turned away with the blade that was already in my hand and stepped out of the weapons room, leaving Zack by himself. Outside the doorway, I caught a glimpse of Renzo and Alura huddled at the far end of the room. Instinct told me their conversation wasn't meant for my ears. Which, naturally, made me want to listen in.

I backtracked until I stood just inside the weapons room again and concentrated on the far corner where Renzo and Alura spoke in hushed whispers.

"Now's not the time," he said hissed.

"Please, Uncle Luc—"

"Shh! Don't call me that."

I froze, my only movement coming from my lungs as they abruptly pulled in air. Had she been about to say Uncle Lucio? As in Zack's father? That would make so much sense—why Renzo had shown up out of the blue and kept watch over us. Was this the secret he'd been keeping?

I saw no point in asking him. Renzo would deny it, same as he had before. And maybe he wasn't related to Zack at all. Maybe I'd jumped to conclusions too quickly and Alura had been about to say something else before being cut off. Maybe all this was wishful thinking on my part so Zack wouldn't be an orphan.

Since I had no proof, I couldn't repeat to Zack what I'd overheard or tell him about my suspicions until I had a confession from Renzo. With everything going down with the vampires, I probably wouldn't get that anytime soon.

Renzo and Alura had quit talking, probably switching to telepathy.

Not loving the idea of explaining to Zack why I was standing inside the doorway of the weapons room, I took a deep breath and entered the training room. When Renzo and Alura glanced over, I waved the sword.

Zack emerged with his own sword a moment later and we split off to our usual teams. I trained hard, until I could smell my own sweat and my muscles quaked. As I forced my body to work harder, my mind drifted. Renzo had a secret—of that I was sure. If the secret was him being Zack's dad, what was keeping him from telling Zack?

† † †

Sweat trickled down my back and I fought for air, wheezing as my lungs strained. From my spot against the wall where I'd landed, I stared up at Alura.

She slapped a fist onto her hip. "You're distracted."

I'd broken up with a guy I was madly in love with and then learned his dad might be right under his nose. Yeah, I was distracted. My eyes automatically searched for Zack and Renzo. I patted the floor next to me and she slid down.

I overheard you and Lucio talking earlier. I hit her with a smug look, one brow up.

Her whole body jolted and she pulled back, her gaze flitting back to Renzo for an instant.

After that reaction, any lingering doubt in my mind had totally dissipated. *Glad you're not going to try to deny he's Zack's father.*

"No. I'm not." She dropped her head against the wall. *I don't want to lie anymore. I've been trying to get Uncle Lucio to tell Zack from the beginning, but he keeps saying it's not time yet.*

Despite Renzo's denials over him being Zack's dad, I'd actually nailed it weeks ago. Shock had my lungs emptying. I quickly composed myself, not wanting to draw Zack's attention. *What is he waiting for?*

He wants a real relationship with his son. The last thing Uncle Lucio wants is for Zack to be cooperative just because he's his dad. The problem is my uncle never believed he deserved Favianne's love, and he deserves Zack's even less. And since he's been gone all this time, he believes he needs to earn Zack's love and respect.

But he already earned Zack's love when he was small, I said, remembering Zack's expression anytime he'd talked about Lucio.

She offered me a tight smile. *That's what I keep telling him. But he has so little experience with kids and he usually doesn't know what to do. I'm sure you've noticed he's not a warm and fuzzy kind of guy. It's going a little slower than he expected, but he's trying.*

I guess that makes sense. I sighed. *But I hope he doesn't wait too long.*

It's already been too long. She bumped my knee with hers. *In a day or so, he'll have no choice but to tell him.*

My head snapped up. *What about Favianne? Was Renzo able to see her before she died? Was that why he was at the hospital?*

She nodded, her head angling down. *Yeah, that's why he was there. I only wish he'd been able to change her into a werewolf.*

Me too. But I couldn't think about Favianne. And Zack losing her. Dwelling on that made me sad and threw me off course. "She was pretty awesome. I miss her."

Renzo loomed over us, scowling. "No one informed me it was break time."

I scrambled to get up and Zack appeared, giving me a hand. Against my better judgment, I let his fingers wrap around mine. Tingles swept over my skin and as soon as I was vertical again, I stuffed my hand in my pocket.

"Everything okay?" he asked.

Yes! His dad was alive and soon he'd know it. I squashed the urge to tell him, pressing my lips together so the words didn't sneak out. "Yeah, all good."

"Let's get back to work," Renzo bellowed.

What was with Renzo? If he wanted to reconnect with Zack, why was he almost always such a tool? Ordering us around and being grumpy wasn't going to give us the warm fuzzies.

Zack glared at Renzo. I hoped our fearless trainer improved his parenting skills soon. If Zack joined SWAAST as he planned, then Renzo would be both his dad and boss. If he kept pissing off Zack, I couldn't see how that was going to work.

Now I understood the importance that Renzo put on establishing trust with Zack since they would be heavily dependent on that in the future. If he didn't end up alienating Zack completely. I needed Zack safe with SWAAST, not on his own.

On the downside, any association with SWAAST painted a bull's-eye on him. But being a part of a group might provide some kind of backup. All the more reason for him to make nice with Renzo.

Two hours later, we stopped for dinner. My face steamed from heat and sweat, and my hair stuck to my neck. Though my body healed quickly and I never endured muscle aches for long, my energy had been thoroughly drained.

"Are we training after dinner or taking a break?" I asked between bites of roasted vegetables. "Because if we're going to get attacked tonight, I'd like to save my strength."

Renzo gave us a small smile. "You two are coming along all right. You won't win any championships, but any vampire who messes with you will get way more than he bargained for."

"Uh-huh." I aimed a finger at him. "You didn't answer my question."

He muffled a laugh. "There are a couple of tricks I want to show you. Then I'd like you to spend the rest of the evening on vampire debrief before our run tonight. The more you know about them, the better you'll handle yourself in battle."

My stomach twisted at the thought of our run in the woods later. That was the obvious place for the vampires to ambush us since we were out in the open.

"Why don't we morph in here later?" I asked. "Maybe we could practice sneaking in bites without getting fangs in us and being bled dry. This way, we'd get our shifting urge out of the way and we won't be going into the woods to make ourselves vulnerable."

Renzo pursed his lips thoughtfully. "Not a bad idea."

Alura jerked her head toward the weapons room. "Zack, help me put the swords and daggers away."

"What's she up to?" Renzo's eyes narrowed at Alura as she and Zack disappeared through the door.

Good question. Was she leaving me alone with Renzo on purpose so we could discuss fatherhood? While I wasn't crazy about him, he wasn't such a bad guy. At least he was here for his son. But I didn't get why he had wasted so many precious moments letting Zack think he didn't have a father.

Then again, if I had come back from the dead and my own son didn't recognize me, I'd want to wait until we were both ready. I'd want to do it right. I hoped Zack lived long enough for Renzo to drop that bomb.

So... when are you going to tell Zack you're his dad? I asked.

Renzo pivoted slowly and opened his mouth to speak.

Don't bother trying to correct me. I heard Alura call you Uncle Lucio. I let that sink in. She didn't deny it. I think she's tired of covering for you.

His face reddened with fury. *And now I'm at your mercy to keep my secret?*

I groaned, my patience waning. *I'm not trying to blackmail you. I just need a good reason to be silent for you when Zack could really use a parent now.*

Replace one parent for another? He gave me a look that said I was getting more stupid by the second. *You think too highly of me, Autumn.*

I disagree. A douche bag dad would've forced his way into his son's life, whether the timing was good or not. And a deadbeat dad wouldn't have come back at all. When Renzo merely stared at the door to the weapons room, I barreled on. *He needs to know.*

And he will. Soon. But promise you won't tell him before I do.

I gnawed on my bottom lip. *And when will that be?*

If things go as planned, he's going to find out on his own anytime now, whether I want him to or not.

What was that supposed to mean?

Is Alura really your niece or is that some weird Pretty Woman thing?

He frowned, inclining his head. Apparently, he'd never seen the movie where Julia Roberts pretended to be Richard Gere's niece when she was actually a hooker. Not that I considered Alura anything like a hooker, but the example had worked well in my head when I'd first thought of it.

She's my brother's daughter by blood.

Since she and Zack were first cousins, I'd never again need to be jealous of her beauty and how well they got along. Not that it mattered now that we'd broken up.

Alura and Zack emerged from the weapons room and I immediately got caught up in their debate.

"No way. Vampires are faster. Shape-shifters can't keep up." Alura turned to me. "No offense."

Zack clucked his tongue. "We're arguing over who we'd rather have on our side in a battle—a vampire or a werewolf. But a vampire didn't save Cedric and it wasn't a werewolf either. It was Autumn."

"Fortunately, we have both." She beamed. "Let's get back to work. We'll break shortly to morph and train more, then head up to the suite."

Relief swept through me that we wouldn't be braving the woods tonight. And I couldn't wait to find out more about vampires. I just hoped I'd learn something favorable, rather than more ways they're superior and how easily we could be killed.

† † †

"And here we all are." Cedric's sweep of his hand included everyone in his office. "Please, have a seat."

I plopped onto the settee with Renzo and Alura, while Zack stood on their other side. Beyond him, Tony and Kayla guarded the door. On the opposite end of the room, Dathan stood vigil in his usual spot by the window, and Cedric sat at his desk facing Regis and Braulio.

In my peripheral vision, I snuck a peek at Zack and my heartbeat accelerated. Tears licked at the backs of my eyes as he stared forward like I didn't exist. I powered past the grief and concentrated on Cedric. Stay focused, that's what I needed to do.

"Your Majesty." Renzo stood and glanced around the room. "Autumn suggested we morph in the gym, rather than do the expected and go out into the woods where they might be setting a trap. So that's already out of the way."

"That probably bought us more time," Regis said. "Either way, we've installed extra surveillance in all the common areas of the mansion, including the café, rec room and atrium, as well as around the gym. In theory, the wolves are safe almost anywhere in the building. And while we're protecting them, we can observe our own people."

"Isn't it unlikely the traitors will speak publicly when telepathic communication is a sure thing?" Zack asked.

"Yes," Regis said. "But we can watch for any other suspicious activity."

"We have a list of suspects," Braulio added, waving a piece of paper. "We're watching for anyone sneaking in and out of the estate. We're assuming the others will try to bring in reinforcements since they're down four men. Six total."

"And so we just wait?" There had to be something we could do besides be on the defensive. Unable to keep my limbs still, I clasped my hands together so my fingers didn't tremble. At this rate, I'd be acting like a meth-head shortly.

"Silly, isn't it?" Renzo growled, his gaze cutting to Zack. "We have access to secret tunnels, yet we all stay here like sitting ducks."

"You can leave anytime." Dathan sent Renzo a searing look. "I'll be happy to escort you out."

We'd be free and clear, away from vampires intent on killing us, so long as we weren't tracked. But something about deserting Cedric felt so wrong. We didn't owe him anything. Hell, we'd already saved his life. But he was a good man and there were people out there trying to murder him. And I was supposed to walk away?

Renzo was wrong. I wasn't going to leave, not if there was a chance I could make the difference between Cedric staying in control and utter chaos among vampires.

Zack, I said silently. *The night Cedric was nearly killed and I'd been lying on his floor barely conscious, I vaguely remember overhearing that vampire talk about taking their rightful place in the world. If those guys rule, that could mean danger for every human on the planet. I can't leave yet. I just can't.*

"That won't be necessary, Your Majesty," Zack told Dathan. "We're not going anywhere. Can't we set a trap or something?"

"We've been discussing that," Cedric said. "Unfortunately, any plan we've come up with involves using someone as bait." He regarded the werewolves in the room.

"I'm sure you're all *dying* to volunteer." Dathan glanced over his shoulder at us, his lip curving up on one side.

Renzo had already returned to his seat, but he raised a hand, his eyes flashing to Zack for a split second. "I'll do it."

Zack shook his head. "No way. You're too valuable to SWAAST. I'll be the bait."

Father and son competing to see who gets the chance to get killed? Just because I'd given up Zack didn't mean I could stand to lose him entirely. And I certainly couldn't allow his father to die. Again. "No. I'll do it. I'm the perfect candidate since they probably think I'm a stupid, weak girl. They won't be ready for what I can do."

I could feel Zack staring at me, but I didn't move a muscle. Cedric's lips twisted as he rolled his shoulders. "I don't love the idea, but it'll do."

Crap. I'd get to be the sacrifice. Yay me.

CHAPTER TWENTY-ONE

--- *Autumn* ---

I BRACED MYSELF when waves of anger radiated off Zack and coursed through me.

"Not going to happen," he told Cedric. He'd stepped into my line of vision, his spine rigid. "No one's using Autumn as bait."

For us being broken up, he was being awfully protective. And bossy. Love for him swelled within me, and I fought inwardly to ignore how dry my mouth went just laying eyes on him. I couldn't allow his protectiveness to sway me. I was about to tell him to give it up when Kayla held up a hand.

"Relax, wolves." She sent us each a look that had me closing my mouth and leaning back into the settee. "Your Majesty, the dissidents want what you have—power. The most efficient way for them to accomplish their mission is by gaining control of your wealth and interests, information on witches and werewolves, as well as our database on every vampire in the world.

"But the thing they need most is Dathan's location so they can eliminate him before he's brought out of slumber. Once Dathan is out of the picture, the crown would be ripe for takeover. And right now, the main thing stopping them from having those things is me. I'm your bait."

"Well said, Kayla." Cedric's eyes darted to mine and gave me a tiny nod as if to silently tell me I'm off the hook.

"But ultimately, I'm the one standing in the way, the one they fear most." Dathan rubbed the corners of his mouth, as he contemplated. "Even if they managed to take possession of the palace, they can't be sure of absolute rule over vampires so long as I'm alive.

"I was last seen in Australia seventy-five years ago. Two days is reasonable enough time for Kayla to locate me there, then transport me here. If word should get out of my arrival by helicopter tomorrow evening, we could set a trap on the roof for anyone waiting to attack me."

Regis nodded. "We can hint that we haven't yet awakened you, because we wanted you in a controlled environment for the process, rather than risk you biting anyone. They'll all rush to kill you before you have a chance to wake."

Tony rubbed his hands together as he scooted forward in his seat. "While they think they're hijacking you, we'll be hijacking them."

"That's the plan." Dathan sent us a devious smile. "It might even buy us more time to observe the palace occupants and collect more intel on the traitors." Then, as if finished with us, Dathan turned his back on everyone and faced the window.

We had ten in our army total—three werewolves and a shape-shifter, plus the vampires: Dathan, Cedric, Braulio, Regis, Kayla, and Tony. I figured we stood a pretty good chance. I raised my hand. "If they've lost six of their men and no one can leave the premises or enter, they're probably outnumbered. We can take 'em."

Dathan swiveled from the window to stare daggers at me. "That kind of optimism is what loses a crown."

"At least I'm not so negative all the time," I mumbled. Man, Dathan was a crabby-pants. "I can see why everyone lets you slumber."

One side of his mouth curled up before he turned away again.

"We have some serious disadvantages," Cedric began. "We can't identify the enemy, nor do we know how many there are. We can't be sure when they'll strike or how many others might storm the castle, so to speak. All those factors leave us vulnerable."

"Right," Zack said, "but they're expecting four wolves and three vampires. We have the element of surprise on our side—three extra they don't know about."

"True," Cedric said. "But I'd prefer to take every precaution."

"On that note..." Renzo pushed off the wall. "I thought I'd educate my wolves on the enemy. As in strengths and weaknesses. Perhaps you can provide anything I'm missing."

Dathan spun and like magic appeared in front of Renzo, the fire in his eyes promising violence and daring the werewolf to cross him. "Centuries-old vampire law forbids revealing that kind of information to any other species."

Dathan came off quite terrifying when he wanted to be. And I knew he could back it up with real power. At that moment, gratitude swirled inside me that he was on our side. Sort of.

Renzo stretched taller, going toe-to-toe with Dathan. "And who makes the laws?"

The light in Dathan's eyes grew malignant. "Cedric and I."

"Then change the law, and allow me to protect my own." Renzo's voice gentled. "Cedric asked us not to leave. Help us stay alive so we can fight for you."

"Dathan," Cedric said. "After being around a few centuries himself, I doubt we can tell Renzo anything new. This information is for Autumn and Zack who saved my life. It's the least they deserve."

Dathan growled and returned to staring out the window. I assumed that meant he was giving in.

Cedric leaned back in his chair. "Our weaknesses, let's see... Only the extremely old can withstand the sun and it affects even us, however slight. Amplified emotions but then that's normal for your kind as well." He scratched his chin. "Vampires have a tendency to go mad and kill themselves. That's why truly ancient vampires are rare."

"It's why some of us go into slumber for long periods," Dathan added. "Keeps things fresh."

Hopefully Dathan's recent slumber would keep

him good for a while. We didn't need someone that scary taking a ride on the crazy train. "Can you control humans, like the way we're able to put an idea into their heads?" I asked.

"Yes, but not like werewolves or shape-shifters." Cedric glanced at Dathan who nodded. I guessed this was sensitive information. "While you merely plant concepts or urges, we can make them do anything we want, believe anything, or forget all of it."

"The trick, though," Dathan added, "is that we must make a physical connection. We can only glamour them if we're feeding off them. Are we almost done here?" He scowled at me.

Why direct that my way? Whatever. I wasn't going to let him intimidate me and blow my opportunity to learn more. Who knew when I'd get another chance to pick their brains?

"No." I zeroed in on Cedric and tuned the others out. "How does one turn into a vampire?"

"The human must be drained to the point of death then fed vampire blood within a couple minutes to resuscitate them," Cedric replied. "They'll still appear dead while they are changing. The more blood ingested, the faster the process."

"Which is how long?" Zack asked.

"Anywhere from a few hours if you indulge or a full day if you're limited to a few sips."

So far, they weren't telling us anything we could use. "Do garlic, crosses, and holy water do anything?"

"No, nothing at all." Dathan spun to stare at us.

"Are you finished with the Q and A yet?"

"Not quite." I held up one finger then shifted to Cedric as a low hiss emanated from near the window. What if Dathan turned someone? Would they inherit some of his strength? "Does it matter who turns you?"

"Yes, the strengths and weaknesses of the master are inherited by the fledgling," Dathan answered, spinning to face us again. "Works the same when you're turning a werewolf. If the master is cruel and uncaring, anyone he turns will have that tendency as part of him. It's that much more difficult to control the bad impulses."

Ah, that explained why my ex, Daniel, became so much more violent and creepy after William turned him. "That makes a lot of sense."

"It's why so many werewolves are mean." Tony flinched and averted our gazes. "Not you guys, but you know."

"It's okay." Zack grinned. "We don't care much for the species either. Which is why we're here."

"One more question." I focused on Cedric, knowing this was sensitive info and if anyone would give up the deets, it was him. "If vampire blood heals you, then in theory, a human could live forever on it without ever being turned, right?"

"Only in theory, because he'd be hunted and killed. In the end, anyone who was hijacking vampire blood would end up with a much shorter life than if he'd remained one hundred percent human," Cedric answered.

"So that's a thing?" I asked. "There are people out there who hunt you?"

"They never hunt us for long," Tony said with a harsh tone. "They're called Betweeners since they aren't vampires, but they're not exactly human anymore either. Not while they're amped on vampire blood."

"If you ladies are finished chatting, let's wrap this up," Dathan said through clenched teeth.

Since I couldn't think of any more questions, I rose with Zack and we made a beeline to our bedroom door. *That information wasn't nearly as insightful as I'd hoped it would be.*

True, but we have no idea what might come in handy up the road, he said.

"Uh, Zack?" Cedric glanced up from his cell screen. "You have a visitor."

Who would visit him here? God, I hoped Trevor or Maya hadn't tracked us down. I didn't want my human friends anywhere near a palace full of vampires, especially the ones who were trying to kill us.

"I thought no one was coming or going until this was over," Zack said, a confused look on his face.

"Extenuating circumstances. We've been expecting this one." Cedric vacated the chair and stuck his phone in his pocket. "If everyone would retire to Dathan's room and give Zack some privacy, I'm sure he'd appreciate it. You too, Autumn."

"Werewolf?" I asked.

"No. Vampire." Cedric motioned for me to get up.

Obeying, I glanced over my shoulder at Zack, wondering who the mysterious visitor was. Apparently Cedric felt comfortable having this vampire in the palace, but what could he want with Zack?

Kayla and Tony returned to their post in the hallway outside Cedric's suite and I followed King Cedric, Renzo, and Alura to Dathan's room. "Are these walls sound-proofed too?"

"Dying to see who it is, aren't you?" Cedric chuckled, then lowered his voice. "Yes, all the walls are soundproofed, but we may hear something through the cracks. If not, you'll find out soon enough."

I sat on a chair closest to the adjoining wall and concentrated on the sounds in the next room. Whatever was going on, it was going to be interesting.

Cedric grabbed a book and settled into an overstuffed chair. A moment later, he sat the book on the end table and rubbed his chin as he studied me. "He loves you."

Renzo flinched.

"Zack?" I lifted a shoulder and dropped it. "Maybe. Maybe not."

One side of Cedric's mouth sloped up. "He does."

"We have chaos at the throne and you're discussing puppy love?" Dathan scowled. "You dogs are already invading my suite. How about not compounding your sins with insipid talk? Perhaps not talk at all."

"Even if you two had the real thing," Renzo told me, as though Dathan hadn't said a thing, "doesn't mean you both can't find someone else."

"Also doesn't mean it can't last." Alura rolled her eyes. "Guys, leave her alone."

Good idea since I didn't need to think about Zack's

feelings for me after I'd already dumped him. It was easier to believe his affections for me hadn't run that deep. "He's never said the words. Not once."

"Does he need to?" Cedric asked.

I sighed. "Only a man would ask that."

"Doesn't change the facts." He pressed his lips together, suppressing a smile.

I found myself torn between hoping I hadn't hurt Zack and hoping I had. Because if I had hurt him, then that meant he cared deeply for me. But if he cared that much, what was I going to do about it?

CHAPTER TWENTY-TWO
—— *Zack* ——

CURIOSITY WAS EATING me alive. Aside from the vampires I'd met at the palace, I didn't know any others. But Cedric knew my visitor or he wouldn't have allowed him to come up. And he'd been expecting him. So who the hell could he be and what did this stranger want from me?

I leaned against the arm of the settee, ready for anything, when the patter on the plush carpet outside the suite had me zeroing in on the door leading to the corridor. Soft footfalls, like a woman's.

Kayla opened the door, then slipped out as the guest slipped in. I sucked in a lungful of air. My jaw dropped and my eyes stung.

It couldn't be. Her skin was fresh and young, her color healthy as though she'd never been sick a day in her life. She'd filled out, no longer thin and frail. I shot up from my seat, then froze before approaching slowly. "Mom?"

The younger, more vibrant version of my mother beamed. "It's me, *Tesoro*. I'm okay."

But she'd died. I'd felt it. Positive this couldn't be my mother, I stopped in the center of the room a few feet from her. "That's impossible."

"Yes, impossible." She smiled. "Like werewolves and vampires?"

I inhaled, long and slow. She smelled the same as Cedric and all the other inhabitants in this place. "You're a vampire? Why?"

Her face fell and her cheeks flushed. "Because it was better than dying."

If this wasn't my mother, who could it be? A doppelganger? "It's been six days. Where have you been?"

"In transition. He could only give me a small amount of blood or I'd come back to life and the doctors would have too many questions. So I lay dormant in the morgue for more than a day. When I finally got out of there, I spent the next several days attempting to control my hunger and learning how to be a vampire."

My heart soared at the possibility that I wasn't an orphan after all. I wasn't one hundred percent convinced though. "Why didn't you call me?"

"My sire wouldn't let me." She held her palms open at her side. "It's not uncommon for vampires to be destroyed within the first few days because they can't adjust. I couldn't tell you I was alive and risk you suffering my death all over again. And I couldn't be trusted near humans yet anyway. The more effort I put in controlling my thirst, the sooner I could see you. And then today, I had to wait until the sun went down."

Right—new vampire. No sunlight. I so badly wanted

to believe this was my mother and she was alive. "A few weeks ago, you gave me a black box. What was in it?"

Her mouth widened to expose her teeth, her eyes shining. "Your future without me. Money, bank account numbers, credit cards—everything you'd need if I didn't survive. You didn't want to take it, but I insisted. And then you blackmailed me into going to the doctor."

Sold.

I launched myself at her, picking her up off the ground and spinning her around the room. "I can't believe it!"

She laughed, pushing against my shoulders. "Put me down, silly."

I allowed her feet to touch the floor, but couldn't release her all the way. Not yet. My hands gripping her arms, I leaned back to examine her. "You look amazing. Perfect." Not dead at all. Relief flooded through me. "Yep, being a vampire is way better than dying."

"In most ways." She raised one shoulder. "Took me some time to adjust to the whole blood thing."

I took her hand and tugged her to the settee. Unable to take my eyes off her for fear she'd disappear and I'd discover her being here was a dream, I laced our fingers.

"Who's your sire? And how did he get the task to turn you?" Wait... did she know about me, that I was a werewolf? "How did you find me?"

"Well..." She averted her eyes and licked her lips. "Remember how vague I was about your father's death? I kept the details from you because I couldn't stand the thought of the real images in your head." Her palm covered my cheek. "He was attacked by a bear and dragged away."

However he died, what did it matter now? "What does your sire have to do with Dad being killed by a bear?"

My mom swallowed. "He arranged for an old vampire called Magnus to turn me."

I nodded slowly, not sure if I understood the sequence correctly. "So before he died, he made sure this Magnus vampire would turn you?"

"Uh, no. The bear—shape-shifter—left him for dead, but he survived." Her smile grew wider. "He's alive, Zack. And he saved me. He stood by me through the entire transition."

I froze. Breathe in. Breathe out. Neither of my parents were dead. Which was unbelievable and I couldn't wait to meet him. Except... "Why did he wait so long, Mom. Why?"

"He was badly injured and it took him years and years to heal. By the time he was well enough to blend with humans, you'd already grown up. And I still couldn't be turned into a werewolf because the werewolf virus would've killed me."

"Vampire blood heals. He arranged a vamp to turn you. Why couldn't he use the blood to cure you, then make you into a werewolf instead?"

"Vampires are stingy with their blood, as you can imagine. They'd choose just about any other option before giving their blood to a werewolf. And they rarely make new vampires. But your father was able to get Magnus to glamour my nurse Winnie into putting a few drops into my IV over the years. The vampire blood helped keep me alive, but wasn't enough to totally cure me."

My dad had found a way to save her. I inwardly shuddered, trying not to think about what would've happened to my mom without those drops of blood. No wonder she'd lived beyond the doctors' expectations.

"Yeah, but he's close by. Why couldn't he contact us?"

"Making his presence known to me would mean explaining why he was still alive and what he was. That would put me in danger of being killed since humans aren't supposed to have knowledge of werewolves and vampires."

"Why couldn't he tell *me*, though?"

She hesitated, biting her lip. "He couldn't do that without exposing himself to me. And he couldn't take you away, not without forcing you to abandon me. He didn't want me to lose my child or you to be without your mother. So he spent the last few years searching for a vampire who didn't hate werewolves and would change me. In the end, it was the same vampire who'd given him the original vial."

He'd saved her and that was all that mattered. Anything else he may have done wrong was forgivable. "When can I see him?"

"The thing is..." She gulped. "You already have."

I'd already seen him? She couldn't have been referring to Charles who was dead and buried. I prayed she didn't mean William who'd been run out of town by

Charles. They were perfect, unlikable examples of the werewolf species. But if either were my father, they wouldn't have tried to kill me, right? I hadn't noticed any other werewolves except Renzo and Alura.

"I believe you know him as Renzo Soriano." She eyed me intently.

I sprung from the settee to loom over her. "Renzo?" I growled. "You've got to be kidding."

"*Tesoro*, sit. Talk to me." She patted the spot where I'd just vacated.

I ignored her request, glaring as I paced. "Renzo is my dad? The same Renzo who scared the hell out of us and threatened Autumn? The same guy who's been around for weeks and is now beating the crap out of me every day during training?" I was shouting now and didn't care that everyone, even Renzo, could hear me in the other room.

My mom flew off the couch and bared her teeth. Fangs, actually. She clamped her fingers on my shoulders. "Sit down, Zack."

"No." My hands bunched into fists. "I'm going to find Renzo and kick his ass."

I slipped out of her grasp and made my way to the room where Renzo was probably listening, but in an instant, my mom was blocking my path. "You will not fight your father. I need you to listen to me. There's so much you don't know."

I wouldn't fight her to get to Renzo. I leaned forward and kissed her cheek. "So good to have you back. But I'm sorry. I can't stay. I need some space."

"You can't leave." She sidestepped to stop me and I took that opportunity to get past her.

I barreled through the door, zeroed in on Renzo, and charged. My fist landed in his ribs and he doubled over. "You son of a bitch!"

"Zack!" my mom shouted behind me.

Autumn's mouth dropped open and she stared at my mom with huge eyes. Shaking off the shock, Autumn moved in front of Renzo and blocked me from hitting Renzo again—who hadn't made an effort to defend himself. "Don't do anything you're going to regret."

I struggled to calm myself as I shot Renzo a look of loathing. "All this time and he didn't tell me he was my dad."

Autumn flinched, but she didn't glance at Renzo. As if she wasn't surprised.

Fury raged through me and I rounded on her. "You knew?"

She shook her head. "I just found out a couple—"

"Which means you've had time to tell me." And now I wondered what else she was keeping from me. Maybe her secrets were the real reason she'd broken up with me. Fire burned my brain and streaks of red clouded my vision. "For all your preaching about telling the truth, you're the biggest liar of them all."

"You don't understand." Autumn clung to my arm. "Zack—"

"You have no right to speak me." I shrugged her off. "You're not my girlfriend, remember?"

"Zack, it wasn't her fault and I had my reasons for

not telling you." Renzo rubbed his rib where I'd hit him. "Give me a chance to—"

"Stay away from me! Both of you." I backed out of the room.

"*Tesoro*, listen to them. Please," my mom called out, following me. She'd probably seen me punch the love of her life. Both of them had known for nearly a week that the other was alive and neither could manage to tell me?

The three people I needed most in my life had kept me in the dark. Lied to me.

Unable to look into my mom's pleading eyes, I whirled and headed through the door into the king's study. But I could sense them behind me and I didn't feel like talking. I needed a few minutes to myself, time to think.

At the door to the bedroom Autumn and I had shared, I paused with my hand on the knob. My gaze strayed to the next door over that led to the corridor and beyond. They'd follow me for sure. And somewhere in the palace vamps were waiting to kill us. But if I ran fast enough, they wouldn't be able to see me. They could follow my scent but I'd be over the stone gates traveling faster than they could track me.

Maybe I'd come back tomorrow. Maybe not.

I whooshed out the door, past Kayla and Tony, then bulleted through the house and out the front door. Across the lawn and over the tall stone wall, lightning struck. I convulsed as the violent dose of electricity ravaged my body. My feet stumbled across the top of the wall and I landed on the other side in the soft dirt.

My muscles ached and trembled. Damn Cedric and his security systems. Damn myself for forgetting about them. But I had to keep going or someone might nab me, and it was probably too late to go back. I was already on the other side and vulnerable. Running was my best option—if I was even able to do that.

As I shifted my weight to rocket across the neighbor's lot, something sharp pierced my shoulder blade. Ah, crap. My knees buckled beneath me, but I shot my fists in every direction, hoping they would land on someone. I tried to morph in hopes of using my fangs on whoever had drugged me, but I didn't have enough strength or focus. Even if I had, I wouldn't have been able to stop them from getting the cure. Images swirled and spun around me, and I was plummeting. And then the night sky turned pitch black.

CHAPTER TWENTY-THREE
—— *Autumn* ——

ZACK! COME BACK, *it's not safe.* I waited for a reply, but only silence met me. Somehow, I could still feel our connection. Just like I had sensed when Favianne's human side had died, I would've sensed if Zack had been killed, right? He had to be alive. I tucked my bottom lip under my teeth to keep it from quivering. "He's not answering."

Except for Cedric and Regis who stayed behind to monitor the cameras, we'd all ventured out to the front lawn, sticking close together for safety as we searched the grounds for Zack.

"His scent ends here." Dathan sniffed near the wall, his neck arching so he could smell the air above. "Kayla says he's not showing up on any of the cameras on the other side. She's checking recent footage, but it will take a few minutes to go through them all."

"He's not answering me either. That's not like him." Favianne's hands fisted as she paced. "Doesn't matter how angry he is. He'd at least talk to me, tell me he's fine."

"For all we know, he could already be dead." Tony's gaze darted to Favianne. "Sorry. I shouldn't have blurted that out."

Favianne flinched, glancing at Dathan.

"You may still be too young and weak for consistent telepathic conversation, especially over this kind of a distance." Dathan bounded to the top of the wall and scanned the other side, his body jerking as the invisible force zapped him. He jumped down and shuddered. "That was unpleasant. If Zack escaped over the wall, which appears to be the case with how strong his scent is here, the jolt took him down long enough for someone to capture him. Let's get inside before something happens to one of you."

Panic seized me, my chest tightening. "We won't find him by going back inside."

"Inside. Now," he hissed, pointing at the front door. "I'll explain upstairs. Go."

Everyone moved in unison, our necks craning in every direction in hopes of spotting anyone lurking. But not a soul stirred, as though the palace's occupants knew that now wasn't a good time to be around.

Favianne! In all the excitement, I hadn't had a chance to show her how thrilled out of my mind I was that she was alive. And by the smell of her, she'd been turned into a vampire.

I waited until we'd been safely ushered into the king's suite before I threw my arms around her and held my tears in check. Now was not the time to fall apart. "I can't believe you're here. Missed you so much."

"Not as much as I missed you." She gave me a hard squeeze.

"You'll have time for reunions later." Dathan scowled at each of us until we were all sitting. "Zack's just unconscious. Definitely not dead."

His confidence in Zack's condition caught my attention. "How could you possibly know that?"

"I can sense his state of mind." Facing away from everyone else, Dathan shoved his hands in his pocket.

"But..." Kayla studied him, squinting in disbelief. "There's only one way to get *that* kind of a connection."

Dathan scoffed. "Healing him was necessary in order to catch the culprits who tried to murder Cedric. And then, of course, I required the cure."

"But Zack didn't sustain any major damage. He didn't need emergency healing," Tony said.

I had needed healing though, and Dathan had given me his blood. I waved my palms around the room. "Wait. Does this mean you and I are connected too?"

"You let them *both* drink from you?" Kayla's mouth dropped open. "You've never shared your power with any of us."

"It wasn't life or death." Tony scoffed. "They'd already killed the attackers."

Dathan abandoned his spot by the window and stalked to where Kayla sat. He loomed over her with a glare. "Zack was already wounded and weak when he gave his own blood to save Cedric's life. Preventing Zack from becoming insane with hunger was the least

I could do after his act of heroism."

Kayla slumped under his stare.

"And thanks to his foresight, we have a way to track Zack." Cedric turned to Dathan. "What else can you tell us?"

"Unconscious... and by the strength of the connection, I'd say he's nearby, possibly on the estate somewhere."

Favianne rose from the chair. "You think you'll be able to find him?"

"I believe so. But there's something I need to do first." He strode to Cedric's desk and jabbed his finger into a button. "This is King Dathan, your true king," he grumbled into the microphone. "The young male werewolf has been kidnapped by one of our own."

As Dathan spoke, his voice boomed from the speakers outside the door in the corridors. "Every one of you will be in the training room in five minutes. Those who don't show up will be treated as traitors and killed on sight." He released the intercom button.

"Now what?" Renzo stood. "My son has been taken and the ones who have him very likely aren't on the premises anymore. They sure as hell aren't going to meet with you and leave their captive unattended. So you're going to meet with a bunch of vampires who probably weren't even the ones who took him? We could be using this time to look for Zack."

Dathan's lip twisted. "I'm merely removing obstacles from my path. Since we don't know which of our people are trying to overthrow us, we'll keep the ones here contained while we track Zack."

Brilliant. Another reason to be grateful Dathan was on our side. Apparently Renzo didn't object because he kept his mouth shut.

"Cedric, you stay here and watch the monitors. You're our secret weapon, since they believe you're dead." Focusing on Renzo and Alura, Dathan flicked his hand like they were inconsequential. "Can't have you two ruining this by getting sucked dry by some vampire. You'll be more useful here with Cedric in case anyone tries to gain access to the suite. Favianne, I can't use you without proper training," he told her. "Stay behind with Autumn and help the wolves. Vampires, let's go."

As soon as they filed out of the room behind Dathan, Favianne began to pace. Alura's foot fluttered nervously while Renzo brooded in his chair. I couldn't blame any of them for being restless. Waiting in the king's suite and knowing Zack was out there somewhere, possibly hurt or nearly dead, made me light-headed and my hands clammy. I would rather have been out there with Dathan.

"I hope they bring back some weapons," Alura said. "All I have is this dagger in my boot and a crossbow in Autumn's room."

"Fortunately I keep a supply here in my suite. But we'll get armed in a bit," Cedric mumbled before returning to the monitors.

I loved that Cedric was so badass and always prepared for anything, even having a store of emergency weapons—unlike Renzo, who wasn't badass at all. I made a small effort to hide my resentment while saying, "When we have Zack back, the least you could do is tell him you asked me not to say anything about you being his father. Now he thinks I betrayed him."

"You broke up with him." Renzo's eyes narrowed at me. "What do you care?"

Favianne snapped to attention. "You two broke up?"

"Yes." I jumped to my feet, my arms stiff at my sides as I stood in front of Renzo. "Because you talked me into it. Kept going on and on about the different species thing and how much danger we were in, had me convinced it was the right thing to do." Much to my humiliation, a whimper escaped me. "And then you threw me under the bus."

"You did this, Lucio?" Favianne whispered. "Interfered with two kids in love?"

Renzo hung his head. "Their lives will be a hundred times harder if they stick together. They're young. They'll fall in love with someone else. Maybe someone more appropriate."

"I was about their age when I met you." She knelt in front of him and covered his hand with hers. "When you were gone, I didn't fall in love with anyone else."

"Favianne, it's different with us." He tucked a lock of hair behind her ear.

"What, we weren't different species?" she asked, slanting her head and leaning away from him. "Or are they not the *right* kind of different species?"

A corner of his upper lip turned up. "Maybe it's

not a matter of species, but the right kind of *love*."

"Maybe you shouldn't be the one to judge," she chided, looking down at their joined hands. "There was a time when someone tried to tell *you* who not to love."

Renzo caressed her hands. "She doesn't love him enough. And to be honest, I don't think he cares for her as much as you'd like to think."

"And you know this *how*? You have so much to learn about your own son." Favianne yanked her hands from his, then backed away and sat next to me. "When Zack is back, I'll speak to him," she told me.

I could kiss Favianne for standing up to Renzo. I wanted to do more than that though. The compulsion to morph into a bear and add to his facial scars had me squirming in my chair. Instead, I put that energy toward convincing my eyes not to leak.

I gave her a sad smile. "I appreciate the thought, but he's not any happier with you two."

"He'll come around." She leaned forward and kissed me on the forehead. "I'm sure of it."

"I hope so." I sniffed and raised my chin to check her out more carefully. "You're totally hot, by the way. You could probably pass for a college student."

Her lip twitched. "The perks of quick healing. Our bodies are constantly regenerating and keeping us in our prime."

"Are you three finished?" As soon as Cedric had our attention, he pointed to the monitor. "Dathan is keeping all the vampires in the training room until further notice. Kayla, Tony, Braulio, and Regis will be guarding all exits—obviously Regis's presence is no longer a secret either. That leaves you guys and Dathan to find Zack."

That didn't sound encouraging. "But we have you and Dathan on our side. And these." I tapped my incisors.

Renzo smirked. "We both know your fangs don't have the same bite as ours."

My lip curved up. "I've killed one werewolf and a couple of vamps. With Dathan's blood, after a little more training I could probably take you."

He lifted his lip to show his teeth and leaned forward. "I'll be ready when you want to try me out."

"Lucio, what is wrong with you?" Favianne stuck her hands on her hips. "I'd appreciate you taking less interest in their relationship and more in your own."

"What is that supposed to mean?" He blinked at her from the settee.

"It means that now is not a time for prejudice and clinging to old ideas. We must save our son and once we do, your hostility for the girl he loves won't help rebuild your relationship with him. Or *me*, for that matter." Favianne sighed. "I need you to be the man I know you can be."

That was the second time today someone insisted Zack loved me. Maybe he'd come close to that before I'd dumped him, before I failed to tell him about Renzo. I seriously doubted Zack would ever want me back now. My chest hollowed out at the idea that Zack would want nothing to do with me.

Renzo rose from his seat and stomped toward her. "He's only eighteen and couldn't possibly have any clue what he wants."

"And when I was his age, I got *married*. To you. It's okay for me but not for them?"

A low rumble came from Renzo. I opened my mouth to tell them not to fight over me, that it wasn't an issue because we had broken up anyway.

"Can we stay on topic?" Cedric snapped, his brows pulled down.

Three knocks, followed by another, signaled Dathan's return. The door opened and he glided through the gap. "Let's go get your boy."

CHAPTER TWENTY-FOUR
——— *Autumn* ———

"WE'LL NEED STAKES, tranquilizers..." Cedric marched to the corner of his office where Regis had emerged from the secret tunnel earlier. Just like before, he ran his hand along the wall, pushed, and the door eased open. He disappeared through the doorway, and a light switched on just before he motioned us to follow.

Gleaming metal of every shape—guns and rifles on hooks, crossbows, a variety of blades, and some things I couldn't identify —covered the walls. Zack would've gone nuts in this place. And it was almost as big as the weapons room in the gym.

"How's your aim?" Cedric asked, handing me a crossbow.

"Uh..." I stared at the thing, wondering how I would load it.

"Anything you give her could be taken and used against us. Let her have a dagger for emergency." Renzo nudged the crossbow away. "*She's* our best weapon."

I wasn't sure if that was an insult or a compliment.

"Magnus taught me a few tricks before he brought me here." Favianne eyed the row of swords. "I'll have one of these."

"This one would be good for you." Renzo handed me a long dagger. "No plastic or man-made parts. It'll morph with you."

"Thanks." I cast him a sideways glance, unsure if he was being genuinely nice or setting me up for something.

"Whether you use wood, metal, or plastic, a stake through the heart works the same way," Cedric said, handing stakes to each of us. "These are wood and will morph with you. Be sure to leave them in the heart or the target will heal and, if they get a chance to feed, you'll be back where you started."

"Good reminder." Although I didn't need it. I nabbed a couple of dart-type thingies. "Tranquilizers?"

Cedric nodded. "Yes, it will take out its target instantly and keep them that way for almost an hour. Plastic though. Won't morph with you." He retrieved them from me, then checked his watch. "If they hit Zack with this, right about now is when he should be coming around."

"Running out of time, folks. The longer Zack is gone, the farther away he could get." Dathan shoved a thin knife in his waistband and dropped another into his boot, then chose a crossbow. "Let's go."

Go where? And what if we never found Zack? What if they'd already killed him? My muscles tensed to the point of quivering.

Cedric headed out of the weapons room. I plucked

up a couple of tranquilizer darts and trailed after him. If I were caught in a fight before I had a chance to morph, the darts might come in handy. I stuffed them in my jeans pocket and rushed to catch up with the others.

He stopped before the door that led to the corridor outside his suite. "Dathan, don't let them out of your sight, especially the little one."

"Obviously." Dathan switched to Renzo and Alura. "And, in turn, you two will do the same for Cedric."

"Are you kidding me? I'm going out searching for my son." Renzo attempted to shove past Dathan.

Dathan blocked him. "With my connection to Zack, I'm best equipped to find him. I *will* bring him back. In return, you will stay here and protect what's most valuable to *me*. Make sure Cedric survives." He waited a beat, his jaw tightening. "It's not up for debate."

"You're not my king and you can't stop me."

"His Majesty is right." Favianne laid a hand on Renzo's arm. "Let's do as my king suggests. Please, Lucio. Our son's life is at stake. Please."

Renzo backed off, giving Dathan a curt nod. "Bring my son back alive."

Dathan led Favianne and me out of the suite, paused to make sure Cedric locked up behind us, and then he continued toward the stairs. "Since all palace personnel are in the training room under guard, in theory the rest of the palace is empty. Wouldn't hurt to keep our eyes open, just in case. I imagine word has spread to the enemy and they know we're looking for Zack. They'll be waiting to pick us off."

"Do you think they're holding Zack on the estate?" Favianne whispered. "Or did they grab him and run?"

"He's close by. Obviously using him as bait." Dathan tilted his head toward a room. "They could ambush us at any of the exits. We'll go out through one of the windows, since it's impossible for them to guard them all."

In a matter of seconds, we could be in battle. My body went taut as adrenaline coursed through my veins. "How many vampires are in the gym?"

Dathan grunted. "All but the four guys you killed when Cedric was staked."

I gritted my teeth. "Which means the people holding Zack aren't residents. And we don't know anything about them or how many there are."

"Or how they managed to get back onto the property past the electric-enhanced walls without anyone seeing them." Dathan motioned for us to continue down the corridor and, moments later, halted in front of a door. He turned to me and brushed a few strands of hair from my face. "Relax, little one. We'll find him and he'll be safe again," he said softly, surprising me with his gentle words.

"Okay." I forced a smile. Dathan had earned at least that.

"For now, this is reconnaissance. We'll search the premises and the woods. Once we figure out where they are, we'll back off and formulate a plan." Dathan's eyes darkened and his words took on an ominous tone. "And then we'll slay them all."

And... back to being terrifying. He held the door open and I shadowed Favianne into a pitch-black room.

"As soon as we're out there, silent communication only." Dathan carefully slid the window up and held an index finger across his lips. *You two go first and I'll be right behind you. Remember, no noises. You don't exist.*

I could do that. I'd snuck in and out of Zack's bedroom for months.

Once outside, the three of us crept behind the bushes, inching along as we peeked past the leaves. *I don't see anything,* I told them.

Don't forget about your other senses. You must listen for unusual sounds, check for unfamiliar scents. And you should try Zack again; check if he's awake.

That's assuming he'll answer me. Something flickered in the distance.

I doubt his anger with you overrides his desire to be free from his captors, Dathan pointed out.

I aimed an index finger in the direction of the tiny light that had since gone out. *Did you see that?* They shook their heads and I clenched my jaw in frustration. *It was a light from over there.*

We'll check it out. Dathan nodded. *In the meantime, try him again.*

Zack, we're coming for you. Do you know where you are?

No, I was unconscious when they tied me up. But you need to stay away. There are too many of them.

Zack was alive! Relief flooded through me. *And if I*

was the one surrounded by crazy vampires, could you walk away? His silence was my answer. *I didn't think so. Where are you?*

I have no idea.

How many vampires are there?

Ten, maybe fifteen.

Against us three. Awesome. I swallowed hard and slipped one hand into Favianne's, and the other into Dathan's, so they could hear our conversation. *About fifteen vampires,* I repeated for their benefit. *Do you recognize any of them?* I asked Zack.

You shouldn't come.

Dathan and the rest of them won't leave you. Neither will I. Now tell me if you recognize anyone around you.

I don't. But everyone here is taking orders from Francois. I think his last name was... Thomas maybe.

Ah, yes, Dathan said. *Very old vampire who supposedly died decades ago. Did they mention anyone else? Maybe they talked about someone who had been there but left before you woke up?*

They mentioned Vincent... or maybe that was his last name. Pierre or something like that. I don't know. They needed him a few minutes ago, but he's in the palace, I think. I'm a little fuzzy from whatever they used to knock me out.

If you think of anything else, let us know, Dathan told him as he gave my hand a brief squeeze. *Hang in there. We'll find you, I promise. Cedric, have Braulio and Regis bring Pierre Vincent up to your suite. He was with Zack's kidnappers.*

My pleasure, Cedric returned. *I'll let you know whatever I learn.*

No one can torture information out of an enemy the way Cedric can. Dathan released my hand and pointed at the stone wall. *Meet me there. Now.*

Cedric was badass, for sure. But having the balls for hard-core torture? I zoomed across the lawn, meeting Favianne and Dathan. *Cedric tortures people? I can't imagine that being his thing.*

I didn't say he liked it. He indicated another section along the wall. *Only that he's good at it.*

That was a little creepy. But I was beginning to see creepiness as the norm for so many vampires. Dathan's gaze darted toward another spot and we whizzed there.

Before he could move again, I grabbed his arm and Favianne's hand. *Do you sense Zack stronger? Because I have his scent.*

Me too, Favianne said.

He's close by. Dathan stood motionless for a moment, like he was trying to get a read on Zack. *You two stay here while I check it out.* His eyes warned me not to disobey.

I sent him a hard look. *We'll stay, but come back soon or we're coming after you.*

He snorted. *Big talk from a rookie shape-shifter.* And then he was gone.

Favianne rubbed my arm. *We'll find him.*

After what felt like five full minutes, my nerves were

frayed from straining my ears to listen for Dathan's return. The hairs on my neck tingled as I imagined the worst.

I'm on my way back, Dathan pushed into my mind, and relief poured through me.

He reappeared seconds later. *Zack's tied upside-down swinging from a tree. Aside from some dried blood from old wounds, from what I can tell he's fine. Several vampires guarding him, but I have a feeling more were hiding nearby.* He waited a beat. *They'll attack as soon as we attempt to free him.*

Of course they would. *Can't we skulk around the property and pick off the vamps one by one?* I asked.

Dathan threw me a lopsided grin. *That's what I was thinking.*

I'd never actually gone on the attack. Zack and I had been in more than one battle for our lives, but we'd always been defending ourselves. Or defending Cedric. To neutralize the vampires, I'd need to stalk them like prey with intent to kill.

I clenched my jaw, reminding myself that Zack's life was at stake. From the same group who had tried to murder their king. To save Zack, I'd do it. But my fingers twitched uncontrollably and I balled them into a fist.

I'll be the one killing vampires, Dathan clarified. *Not you two. I'll escort you both back to Cedric's suite.*

Sure, I was terrified. But that didn't mean I was going to chicken out and risk Zack dying while I stayed safe and comfy in the royal suite. *Why did you bring us if you were only going to send us back?*

Because we had no idea what we were dealing with and I thought your eyes and ears might come in handy. And I was right. He clamped onto my arm. *You're going back and you're letting me handle this.*

As Dathan yanked me toward the estate, rustling from nearby pulled my attention to Favianne trailing close behind. Dathan spun, throwing me aside, and I stumbled back. I gasped as a vampire sprung at Favianne and staked her in the heart. She crumpled and the vampire lunged for Dathan.

CHAPTER TWENTY-FIVE
─────── *Autumn* ───────

MY MOUTH WATERED with the need to vomit as the vampire collapsed and Dathan tossed his heart on the ground. As several other vampires surrounded us, Dathan shielded me.

"Cowards," Dathan told them, backing up so I had to as well. "Six against two isn't a fair fight, is it?"

Maybe I'd exaggerated Dathan's abilities in my mind. There were six of them, after all. I couldn't depend on him. Not when Zack's, and now Favianne's, life was in grave danger. I morphed into a wolf, knowing they believed me to be a werewolf and they'd want to avoid my teeth.

"Which of you will be first to die of a werewolf bite, hm?" Dathan sneered. "Or the next to get their heart ripped out." He stared at them hard. "Do you have any idea who I am?"

"Won't matter who you are after you're dead." The olive-skinned vampire advanced with a smirk.

Dathan reached out and shoved his hand into the vampire's chest while using him as a shield. "I'm your worst nightmare."

The vampire's eyes went blank and he toppled onto the body of the other vampire. Dathan tossed the heart behind him, splashing me with droplets of blood. I suppressed the revulsion and resumed my snarling.

The other five vampires hesitated a split second before they vanished. I morphed back into my human form, then reached down and plucked up the tranquilizer darts that hadn't morphed with me, shoving them back in my pocket.

"Let's get back inside." Dathan wiped his bloody hands on his jeans and scanned the area for any other vampires. Then he kneeled down, pulled the stake from Favianne, and scooped her up.

"Cedric, are we clear to come inside?" he mumbled, obviously talking simultaneously aloud and silently. He paused at the window, his back to the wall. "This was a horrible plan."

"Cedric didn't answer?"

"No. Which means we don't know if the palace has been compromised."

Favianne moaned. "Put me down."

Dathan muttered quietly, but complied. "Feed her," he demanded. "Since we can't get to blood bags right now."

How could she be talking so soon after being staked? "Did they miss your heart?"

"Yes." She grimaced like she was in pain. "But they still did a fair bit of damage."

I offered my wrist. "Drink. Or you won't be able to

protect yourself."

"Apparently protecting myself isn't my specialty or I wouldn't have been stabbed." She eyed the vein at my wrist and swayed backward. "I'm new at this and can't vouch for my control. Stopping may be difficult, and I can't risk you getting weaker."

Dathan snorted. "That's assuming Autumn is weak and can't stop you. She's not and she can."

He almost sounded protective of me. Even a little proud. I hoped his faith was well placed, because I had my skin to save, not to mention Zack's and now Cedric's.

"I can't feed from you, Autumn." Favianne nudged me away.

"You will if it means you'll heal and get stronger." I inched my wrist closer to her, but she merely tilted her chin up. Damn, we needed to get her inside and straight to the blood supply. "How long are we going to stand here by the window?"

"We're already surrounded." Dathan spread his arms as if to hold me back. "But since they can't guarantee a win against me, they're waiting for the rest of the gang before they attack." He probably didn't care if the other vampires heard him or he would've spoken to me silently.

I couldn't help wondering if Cedric had been wounded or worse. And what about Renzo and Alura? I laced my fingers through Favianne's so she could be a part of the conversation I was about to have with Renzo. Before I had a chance to call for him, Dathan bumped a shoulder against mine and spoke silently.

Kayla, Tony, everything okay over there?

All our people are still locked in, Kayla answered. *Braulio and I, Regis, and Tony each have a side of the building. And His Majesty is prowling around checking cameras and sensors. Although, for the record, I advised him not to leave the suite.*

He's not answering us, I told her. *Once you find him, let us know.*

You're handling yourself admirably, by the way. Dathan flashed me a crooked smile. *We'll make a warrior out of you yet.*

Not my lifelong dream, but it'll keep me alive. I returned his smile.

Are you guys okay? Cedric asked. *Had a couple of intruders sneaking in through the vent into the gym. They spotted me. Renzo and I were busy neutralizing them before they could tell anyone else I'm not really dead.*

Why aren't you on the monitors? Dathan asked.

Because someone took out a bunch of them. The working ones aren't getting any action. I'd steer clear of the rear and west side, by the way.

Too late. *We're already at the rear and they're coming for us at any moment,* I said.

I can come out of hiding if you can't handle them on your own, Cedric volunteered.

No. Dathan fired off a stern look at me, warning me not to encourage Cedric. *We need you back in your suite where you can protect everything in it. If we lose that, we could lose the throne.*

Our throne isn't more important than the lives

we're protecting, Cedric hissed into our heads.

Dathan stood rigid next to me. *But if we don't have a throne, it will be much harder to protect them, now or centuries from now. Not to mention the humans. Think long term, my friend.*

I'll be back in my chambers in no time, Cedric replied.

Let me know when you're back inside, or I'll have to abandon my mission and come after you. Even speaking telepathically, Dathan sounded formidable.

"What's the plan?" Favianne asked, swaying where she stood.

The plan is for you to feed off the next vampire stupid enough to cross me. Dathan inhaled, sniffing the air. *Which is right now.*

A whole swarm of them came out of nowhere, fast approaching. Damn! They must have disabled the electrical barrier on the walls. I morphed into a wolf, teeth bared and snarling, snapping at the closest vampire who was wielding a stake. He missed my heart, but the stake sank into my shoulder. The wound stung like hell.

I avoided his next attempt by slipping between his legs to get behind him. I propelled myself up and onto his back, my jaws aiming for his neck. He spun, trying to shake me, and I clung harder.

Ahead of me, Favianne was feeding from the neck of a headless vampire—gross. After wiping her mouth, she rose, unsheathed her sword, and vaulted toward one of the vampires dancing around Dathan. He was fighting off at least six of them, swatting them off like bugs, then using the ones he'd wounded as a weapon against others. Bodies were flung away, but they kept coming back.

Behind me, footfall pounded the grass and I knew more were coming. I had to take this guy down now, but I wasn't sure how quickly I could sever his head in my wolf form.

I morphed back to my human form. In one fluid motion, I pulled the stake from my waistband and, aiming for his heart, I stabbed him in the back. The vampire wheezed and collapsed.

As I vaulted toward Dathan, I glanced at the vamp I'd dropped when Favianne sliced her sword through the air and the blade came crashing down on his neck. Using the tip of her sword, she nudged the head away from the body.

Dathan had killed three more vampires, but he had several more to contend with. Favianne fended off two vamps at the same time, slashing her sword through the air at lightning speed so they couldn't get close.

In my peripheral vision a mob advanced on us. No way could we fight all of them, not even with Dathan on our side. *More just arrived. We need to retreat!* I said.

Can't. Nowhere to go. He shoved his fist into another vampire's chest and extracted the heart, then shoved the body of the vampire aside and moved on to the next one.

I whipped a knife from my waistband and plunged it into the back of one of the vamps toying with Favianne, sure I'd hit his heart. He went wobbly, then slowly plummeted to the ground.

When the other vamp around Favianne glanced over for only a split second to see what happened, she took her opening and swung her sword. His head barreled toward me and I ducked, circling around and coming face-to-face with the mob of vampires. I morphed into a wolf, baring my teeth and growling to keep them at bay.

If they're all here, I'm betting very few of them are watching Zack. Now is the time. Do what you do best, shape-shifter, Dathan told me as he flicked off another vamp. *Go!*

What I did best was morph into a bear and do some damage. But Dathan wasn't asking me to stay and fight. He was telling me to go. Should I abandon Dathan and Favianne though? She was swishing her sword so quickly that no vampires dared come near her. But eventually one would get past the sword. If she died again, how could I tell Zack I'd deserted her?

We'll handle these guys. This could be our best chance to get Zack. Go, little one!

Dathan's past douchiness didn't change the fact that he was brilliant in strategies and battles. Now was probably not the time to doubt him.

Keep Favianne safe! I told him. Snapping and snarling, I backed up. Ten vampires advanced on me. Oh, hell, I had no idea how I'd get away. I could morph into a bird but then they'd know I wasn't a werewolf.

Go. I'll make sure none of them follow you. Dathan hurled a dead vamp in front of me, distracting my attackers for a fraction of an instant—long enough for me to vanish.

After returning to my human form, I bolted in the direction of the woods. Not far behind me, branches whipped and cracked. No way could I allow the vamps to tail me or I might never get the chance to rescue Zack. I leaped high up into a tree and sat deathly still on a thick branch in hopes of taking the vampire by surprise—if he didn't smell me.

He slowed as he neared the tree trunk below, and circled as he surveyed his surroundings, then he looked up. Crap, how was I going to get out of this?

A wicked grin split his face. "Come on down, sweetheart, or I'm coming up after you."

Then his body went slack, his chest jutting out. His eyes lost focus as he toppled to the soft earth.

Dathan stood in the vampire's place and tossed the bloody heart over his shoulder. *Keep going. And be careful.*

If he was here, where was Favianne? All I could do was hope she was safe because I couldn't miss my opportunity to save Zack. Without replying, I dropped to the ground and tore across the lawn to where I'd stopped earlier with Dathan and Favianne.

I drew air through my nose, but didn't detect any vampires. Knowing about them wouldn't do me any good though, since the moment I sniffed one out, they'd smell me too. Crap.

The only way I could successfully rescue Zack was if I didn't give them a chance to sense me. I had to get in and get out. Which meant I couldn't waste time figuring out his exact location.

Dathan, where specifically is Zack? I don't want to go in there blind and get killed before I ever find him.

There's a clearing all the way in the back near the rear entrance. He's hanging from a tree, so make sure you have a dagger on you to cut him free.

I gulped. I had to locate Zack, rescue him, and then get us both away before the vamps spotted me. That was assuming Zack was strong enough to move on his own, otherwise his extra weight would slow me down. It seemed like an awful lot to accomplish without getting killed. But I couldn't give up now. No way would I leave Zack. *Cedric, do you have cameras near the back gate?*

No. They've all been taken out.

Crap.

I soared to the wall and scanned the area where Dathan said Zack would be. But I wasn't high enough to see anything but a thicket of leaves and branches.

I pushed off the wall and took flight, aiming for a humungous tree. I climbed to the top and pinpointed the clearing. Zack wasn't in my line of vision, but there were several other vampires spread out over several yards. I guessed Zack to be right about in the middle.

The only form I could take that would give me enough strength to protect myself was a bear. But I needed to hold the dagger with human fingers to cut Zack free. I couldn't be both forms simultaneously. Even if the branches could hold my weight as a bear, taking the time to morph after I untied Zack wasn't an option either, because it took a couple of seconds to change—more than enough time for any of them to decapitate me.

If I couldn't protect myself while handling Zack's ropes, I couldn't save him. Terror gripped me and my chest felt like it would explode as I scaled down the tree and returned to the wall. I crouched at the top, working up the nerve to storm their campsite.

From my vantage point, I could see a lone vamp pacing along the back wall near the gate.

What if I took them out one at a time?

Drawing a deep breath and releasing it, I prepared myself for attack. For *murder*. I'd killed Charles weeks ago in self-defense, but the idea of purposely going after a vampire with the intention of ending his life had me flinching.

But I *had* to kill him. If I didn't, we'd have to deal with him later and that could mean the difference between getting out alive or not surviving. And the longer I waited, the more time they had to hurt Zack.

I had an instant to neutralize the nearby vamp. I could try to stake him, but what if he fought me? I could end up being staked instead. I could attack him from behind and keep myself out of his reach.

But if I missed on the first try, then I'd have to cling to him while trying to aim for his heart. And while I'm struggling to get the upper hand, he could beat me to it. Too risky. Any hesitation on my part would give him a chance to overpower me.

I'd have to knock him out first. Paralyze him

another way.

I waited until he was closer and when he turned away, I rocketed along the wall and hopped on his back. With my legs firmly gripping his middle, I clamped a hand onto his jaw with one hand and his forehead with the other.

Just before I wrenched his head all the way around, his hand reached up and struck blindly at me with a knife, slicing my upper arm. His neck cracked and we tumbled to the ground. He lay motionless, but I knew that might last only a matter of minutes.

Snatching the dagger from his hand, I used all my strength to stab him in the neck. He awakened and struggled beneath me, but I kept carving away and he weakened with each tendon and vein I severed. When I was halfway done, he flopped then stilled over the grass.

Clenching my jaw and swallowing back vomit, I glanced around to make sure I hadn't been spotted, then returned to my task. His eyes stared up and he twitched until the last tendon and vein had been severed. Shuddering, I rubbed my stinging arm then tossed his head away from his shoulders.

Wiping the tears that had dribbled down my cheeks, I vaulted up to the wall again. I doubted I could get any closer to Zack without someone seeing me. I'd have to turn into a bear, charge the place and kill any vampires standing in my way, then I'd morph into a human and free Zack from the ropes.

And probably get killed in the process.

CHAPTER TWENTY-SIX
—— *Zack* ——

LEAVING CEDRIC'S SUITE had been an idiot move. As soon as I'd been electrocuted at the top of the estate wall, I'd been hit with a dart. I'd woken later already bound, gagged and hanging upside down.

When the vampires had realized I was conscious, a couple of them started using me as a punching bag. They swung me back and forth, taking turns messing me up, then finally handing me over to a vampire they called Dennis.

He'd fired off a few blows at me and broken a rib, which then punctured my lung. That didn't come close to the agony I'd suffered when he'd inserted a long, pear-shaped device into my mouth, and then expanded it until I felt my skull ripping apart. It had been indescribably painful.

I so loathed these vampires.

On the upside, they'd been gone a few minutes and I'd had a chance to heal. Except for the current damage being done to my wrists and ankles, which smarted from being tied so tightly. And my shoulders ached from the pressure of the ropes pulling my arms.

Blood from my earlier pummeling leaked into my stinging eyes, and the adrenaline rush of fear had me so amped up I was dying to morph. But I couldn't. If I shifted into a wolf to escape the ropes, they'd slip off my paws and I'd drop into a bed of poison-filled arrows that would have me writhing in pain. And incapacitated soon after.

Zack, I'm close by. How many vamps are with you?

Autumn, I told you to stay away. Saving me isn't worth you getting killed. Whoever came with you can stay. You go back home.

Nope, sorry. We're a little short on help, so it's just me. How many vamps are with you?

Oh, hell no. *Come back later when you have backup.*

Damn it, Zack! How many?

Four. Too many for you to handle on your own.

Yeah, well, I just killed one vamp. Do you see four now or only three?

Right this second I see four. Please, Autumn, don't do this, I begged. Whether she loved me or not, the mere thought of anything happening to her tripled any pain and discomfort I felt.

I'm going to free you first, then I'll need your help. Get ready.

I spun myself in a circle and scanned the area, but didn't see Autumn. She must be behind the nearby wall. I'd placed all four vamps though. Two were huddled together about thirty feet away, murmuring. Dennis paced about the same distance away in the opposite direction. The fourth patrolled the area about twenty away in the direction of the mansion.

The wall about ten feet behind us was unguarded though, and would cover Autumn. Still, any one of them could get to us faster than Autumn could jump the wall and untie me. *Please don't make me watch you die. Go back. Please.*

No way. I'm not leaving you. Thirty seconds, Zack. Be ready.

Another surge of adrenaline spiked through me. Like I needed to be told to be ready. And damn her for not listening.

I wiggled again, spinning myself in another circle. As I came around again, a shadow approached me. She was quiet, I had to give her that. And I'd never been more grateful for her lack of scent. *Last chance. Go.*

Not on your life. Literally. And the next instant, she was up in the tree looking down at me. *Good thing I had all that practice sneaking around, huh?*

Yeah. I gritted my teeth. *I wish you'd had more practice listening. You need to get out of here before it's too late.*

I'm working on it.

Not the way I wanted her to work on it. Stubborn shape-shifter! The branch creaked and my heart stopped. *Autumn, you can't cut me down. As soon as I touch the ground, the crossbows go off on me.*

I won't let you drop, she assured me. *I can't see the vampires from here because of the tree. Are any of them watching you?*

Oh, God, what was she going to do? I rotated again, locating all four of the guards. The two vamps were still huddled like they were in a heated discussion, arms waving emphatically. The fourth guy was still facing the mansion. And Dennis was staring at his cell.

Whatever you're going to do, now's the time. Just don't let me fall into the arrows.

I felt a tug on the rope and the crossbows gradually got farther away. Lifting my head up, I could see Autumn straining as she heaved me higher by the rope. About halfway, she stopped and left me dangling and twirling.

I twisted to get a bead on the vamps again. They only needed to glance my way and we'd both be killed before I ever reached that branch where she could untie me. My pulse accelerated. *What's wrong?*

I ripped open a wound. Give me a second.

A second we couldn't spare.

My body began ascending again, but slower this time. And then, once again, I halted mid-air. My pulse hammered in my throat and panic swept through me. This was a disaster. Autumn was hurt and she was spending her last bit of energy rescuing me. And then I'd have to carry her away. I wasn't sure I had enough strength to save her, save myself, and fight off four vamps.

At last the toe of my shoe touched the branch above me. She wound the extra rope and knotted it around a broken limb, then reached down to slip her fingers under the ropes around my chest that were binding my arms to my side. Her other hand looped onto the waistband of my jeans and she hauled me up. As I lay over the branch, face down on my stomach, she freed me of the ropes on my wrist.

While she got to work on my bound ankles, I rubbed the raw skin and peeked down at the cross-bows that were all set to shoot. The vampires were still preoccupied. But they were bound to look my way soon and then we'd be in for a battle. I wanted to hug Autumn—among other things—but we didn't have time for sappy reunions. Not that she'd be recep-tive anyway. I tamped down my disappointment and focused on getting to safety. *How bad is it?*

Autumn followed my gaze to her arm and she shrugged. *It was a deep wound and that threw me. But it's healing, I swear.* She fished a dart from her pocket and a dagger from her waistband, then handed them to me.

I knew what to do with them. *Go jump the wall,* I told her. *I'll be there in a minute.*

The wall? The house is the other direction. Any second they're going to notice you're missing. We don't have time for a detour and you need to heal before taking on any battles.

All I've been doing on that rope is healing. What I need to do won't take long. I pointed toward the wall.

She glided soundlessly down the other side of the tree, avoiding the crossbows, then I followed. Dennis was a few yards away with his back to me. As stealth-ily as possible, I flew across the grass toward him. He rotated and I pierced his heart with the dagger.

That's for torturing me, you sick son of a bitch, I told him, taking a moment to mentally prepare myself to cut off his head. But Autumn had a handful of his hair and was already slicing away at his neck. Disgusting.

Hadn't she told me a few minutes ago that she'd already killed a vampire before she got to me? A week ago, I would've followed Autumn straight to the estate after being rescued, not stopped to kill a vampire, even if he had tortured me.

Killing had never been so easy. What the hell had happened to us?

Dathan.

When she'd severed the bone and carved away the last piece of flesh, she knocked the head aside. I yanked on her hand, dragged her to the block wall, and we jumped to the other side. I kept hold of her hand as we ran through the nearby estate and past the next.

We were far enough away now. I slowed to a stop and she turned to me. "It's Dathan's blood," I said.

"What do you mean?" A pucker formed between Autumn's brows.

"When you killed Charles, you were in an animal form. Much easier to kill. I'm not saying it's easy right now, but it's not nearly as hard as it should be."

Her face warped into a grimace. "By drinking his blood, he gave us the ability to kill. Not that we couldn't before. There's just less guilt now."

"Yeah, although I'm not sure if that's a good thing or bad. We need to get back to the palace," I said, wondering what other interesting qualities Dathan had passed on to us. I hoped I wouldn't become a tool. "Is my mom okay?"

"Last time I checked, yeah. She was with Dathan, holding her own."

"Good." Afraid I'd lose Autumn as we ran, I gripped her hand and tugged, then paused mid-step. "Before we go back, let's take out that other guy by the gate. Then later, we only have to deal with two of them."

"You nab, I stab?" She waved her dagger.

"Gross, Autumn." I wanted to kill Dathan for changing my girl into a cold-blooded killer. Except she wasn't my girl anymore.

"You started it." She rolled her eyes. "Let's get him."

After sprinting back toward the cluster of trees, we stopped at the wall that led back to Cedric's estate. We pulled ourselves up and hung on the edge by our elbows while we searched the area for more vamps.

Where are you guys? I asked Dathan, scanning the distant grounds. *We have one quick thing to do and we're heading back.*

"Nice job, you two, but they're all either gone, paralyzed, or dead." Dathan smirked up at me from below. "We captured one of the guys who were holding you here, but another one ran off," he said. "Braulio and Kayla have several locked up in the basement awaiting interrogation. Maybe we can find out who else was in on it. Maybe not. Regardless, I believe it will be a while before they build up their army and resources adequately to make another move against us. For now, it's over and you guys are free to go home."

I couldn't wrap my head around how casual Dathan sounded about it all. "Someone who betrayed you is running loose out there, but you're calling it a day? Doesn't sound right to me."

Dathan scoffed. "They wouldn't be the first to gain trust in order to take the crown. There will *always* be others who work toward our demise, and the palace will never be one hundred percent loyal. We do the best we can and have contingencies in place when we need it. That's all we can do."

"Fair enough." Autumn jumped to the other side of the wall. "This obviously isn't your first time surviving an attack like this."

"No." His mouth curved up. "But it's the first time I had help from the rival species we were fighting."

"My mom okay?" As I swung my body over the wall and eased down, it occurred to me that she wasn't the only family. "What about my dad and cousin?"

"Everyone's fine." Dathan surveyed the area then stretched out a hand to me. "And now Cedric isn't alone in his debt to you."

"Not you too." I flashed a palm at him. "You guys offered asylum and we took it. Clean slate."

"Whatever you say." Dathan nodded at a nearby headless body. "We have some bodies to dispose of."

"Oh." Autumn's mouth twisted. "That sounds super fun."

I exhaled in relief. She wasn't too hard-core if the dead still revolted her.

"Zack!" My mom jogged across the lawn and tumbled into my arms. "Oh, baby. I'm so glad you're okay."

"Yeah, I'm good. But when the dust settles, we should talk." I breathed in her sweet, metallic scent, then gave her one last hug before releasing her.

"Yes, we have much to discuss." She gave me her mom smirk that told me I was going to get reamed. What the hell? *She* was the one who'd kept secrets from me. I was the one who had the right to be angry, not the other way around.

Autumn threw herself at my mom. "You're alive. Again."

"Yeah, yeah, let's go." Dathan waved a hand toward the palace. "Before one of the unconscious decides to wake up and dart us with tranquilizers."

CHAPTER TWENTY-SEVEN
—— Autumn ——

BY MORNING, WE'D almost finished matching the bodies to the heads, identifying them, and logging the info into the database. Those tasks would never make it to my Top Ten Fun Things to Do, but at least I wasn't the one hauling all the bodies to the basement incinerator.

From what we could gather from the interrogations Cedric had conducted, only two of his palace staff—other than the four who'd died while trying to assassinate him and the two we'd captured who'd staked Kayla and Tony—had been involved with the kidnapping. The rest of the bodies hadn't been palace residents.

Once the estate had been restored to normal, those of us who'd been up all night took some time to catch up on rest. I stopped to check in with my parents so they'd know I was okay. And Maya of course. After hearing the relief in her voice, guilt smothered me for disappearing on her. Zack called his aunt Cara and assured her he was fine, promising to be back soon for Favianne's memorial service in two days. I wished

I could tell them Favianne was alive. But I couldn't.

Later that afternoon, I gathered with Zack and his family in the gym, along with the king's council. Dathan stood next to Cedric on a makeshift stage.

The place was packed with vampires from all over the city. They spilled out of the gym and into the atrium.

The table had been placed in front of Cedric and I wondered why they'd set it up with a goblet and knife. Maybe they'd rooted out someone in the audience who had been a part of the uprising and they planned to make an example of him in front of the rest?

Cedric was finishing up his summary of recent events while he made eye contact with various vampires in the crowd. "To my staff, who stayed in this room as we dealt with the traitors, I thank you. To apprehend those responsible for the kidnapping, it was necessary to isolate you in order to prevent confusion between you and those who would eventually be killed or captured."

Murmurs floated through the large room and one vampire stepped forward. "If I may speak for everyone, we are grateful that the news of your demise was false." He bowed and stepped back with the others.

Cedric nodded. "We have the werewolves to thank for that. They wanted to leave almost as soon as they arrived, but I persuaded them to stay and help. They showed great courage and risked their lives so that I might discover those behind the threat to the throne."

A blond woman stepped forward. "Do we have any more information on the attacks in Arizona, Montana, and New Mexico?"

Cedric shook his head. "Unfortunately, no. Those crimes appear to be completely unrelated to the unrest here in the palace. Our intel suggests Ulric may be our man. Or werewolf, I should say."

"The werewolf king's henchman?" a blond woman asked as others in the room booed and hissed.

"Yes, his fiercest warrior. And now we know why he's so powerful." Cedric scowled. "We believe he's hunting vampires, using their blood to increase his power to kill his own kind and shape-shifters."

My heart picked up speed. I knew this wasn't the time to interrupt Cedric, but I couldn't help myself. I tugged on his sleeve and whispered, "Is there anyone in particular he's after?" Please not my mom and dad who were in those states around the same time.

His face looked pained. "Your parents have been contacted and are rushing their arrival. We'll go over it then."

My insides iced. This terrifying—and immensely powerful—werewolf could be hunting my parents.

Autumn. Zack nudged me with his elbow. *We'll figure it out, okay? Same way we always do.* Easy for him to say when it wasn't his parents in grave danger. But his words soothed me. I bit back the fear and my limbs steadied.

"As I was saying," Cedric redirected to the audience, "each one of us is indebted to these werewolves, to some degree or another. Specifically Autumn and Zack. I invite all of you to show your gratitude by joining me in a centuries-old ritual."

Dathan stepped forward. "Drinking from a vampire has been illegal for centuries. We outlawed it because of werewolves like Ulric and a few humans. We have no intention of ever revoking this law. However, for tonight only, King Cedric and I agreed to honor these two brave werewolves who risked their lives for us all. His Majesty and I will go first."

The people in the crowd talked amongst themselves and I glanced at Zack. *Are you going to do this?* I asked.

He stared straight ahead. *Haven't decided yet.*

Dathan handed the dagger to Cedric, then held out the goblet for him. Cedric pressed the blade across his wrist and blood streamed into the cup. "For Zack and Autumn," Cedric began, "who without their acts of bravery, I would truly be dead."

Although I appreciated the sentiment, the whole thing seemed exaggerated to me. We'd been fighting for our own lives as much as theirs. Not that I minded the benefits of vampire blood, but taking on their characteristics felt more like acquiring side effects. I didn't want to become more of a killer than I already was.

I laid a hand on Cedric's arm and directed my thoughts to Dathan. *I'm not sure about this. Maybe some aspects of your personality, well, maybe they're not good for me. I'm not comfortable with how easy it was for me to kill.*

Dathan rolled his eyes. *You mean how easy it was to protect yourself when you needed to and how much more prepared you were to fight for your life?* His face grew solemn. *Sharing my power doesn't make you any less of what you are. Your decisions are still yours to make. My blood only makes you stronger and more capable of doing what must be done. Besides, you're not just taking the worst from me and everyone here who's offering. You're taking the best of us as well.*

Does this mean that they'll all be able to keep tabs on me? That was the last thing I wanted.

No, Cedric rubbed his healed wrist on the edge of the cup and the last bit of blood dribbled over the rim and down the inside. *If they were to ingest your essence, yes. But you're not giving anyone your blood. It is they who are giving a piece of themselves to you, which means you'll be able to sense them when they're nearby. And knowing whether a vampire is friend or foe may come in handy.*

I swallowed, noting the other vampires stepping forward to make their offering.

Enjoy this moment, little one. This is the ultimate gift from a vampire. It means they're accepting you into their vampire family as lifelong blood brothers. Dathan turned to the crowd again, cut his wrist, and let his blood stream into the goblet. Braulio went next, then Regis, Tony and Kayla, followed by every vampire in the vicinity.

"Zack, you too." Dathan motioned him to the front and offered him the goblet. "Half of this is yours."

Dathan explained it to me a bit more, I told Zack. *It's okay. I'm going to drink my half.*

Zack hesitantly took the goblet. He sipped, his gaze roaming the room. After a few gulps, he clenched his jaw and slowly pushed the goblet toward me. As he turned away, I imagined how difficult it was for him to put it down. How difficult it would be for me.

Goblet in hand, I braced myself and downed the rest of the blood. I stared at the remaining film on the inside of the cup and stifled the urge to lick every drop. I commanded myself to set the cup down as I studied the faces of the vampires who had participated in the ritual. They were connected to me now. Family. I'd been swathed in a protective cocoon—by my own natural enemy.

Strangely, I was consumed with the hunger to hunt down any werewolf—or any other species—who would dare hurt my friends for their own selfish desires.

Through their blood, they'd passed on to me the instinct and drive to ensure their survival. *Ulric can't feel this connection with those he drinks from or he couldn't slay them,* I told Dathan.

He gave a slight inclination of his head. *A little of our blood has a positive effect on other species. Too much makes you go mad.*

I blinked and refocused on the crowd. Nearly every vampire in the room was bowing their head before Zack and me. My eyes misted and I glanced at Zack. *Wow*, he said.

CHAPTER TWENTY-EIGHT

———— Autumn ————

NOW THAT WE could roam the palace at will, Cedric's council relocated from his private suite to their own quarters. On the off chance that he and Dathan had missed a mutinous werewolf-hating vamp, he wanted Zack and me to sleep in his suite, as well as Alura and Renzo. Since he didn't have enough rooms for us each to have our own, we still had to double up.

Zack hadn't spoken a word to me since the blood ceremony, thoroughly avoiding my gaze at all times. He'd even suggested to Cedric that Alura sleep in the bedroom with me. He commandeered the sofa while Favianne and Renzo took Dathan's room. I didn't know where Dathan had gone but, for all I knew, he could've gone back into slumber.

I shuffled my heavy limbs to bed, rolled over, and allowed the tears to leak out in silence. For the first time in weeks, I'd spent the night without him. I woke after a restless night, more tired than when I'd gone to sleep.

After commanding my body to get out of bed, I

got ready in slow motion, dreading another day of estrangement from Zack. While I caught up with Favianne over breakfast, he was nowhere to be found. Later, I helped Cedric with a computer issue and still no Zack. He popped in close to lunchtime while I was texting my mom, but he was gone so quickly I didn't get a chance to wave hello.

With every hour I endured, Zack was more distant with me. I rubbed my chest, thinking how much further away he'd be by the time tomorrow rolled around. And then it would be time to go. I might never see him again. Would I even get a chance to say good-bye?

I wasn't sure anymore whether or not I'd done the right thing by breaking up with him. But if I changed my mind, what was the point? Zack would probably take off with his parents before I had a chance to fix things with him anyway.

After lunch—which he ate in another part of the palace—Zack left for a walk with his mom and dad to talk things out. Too queasy to eat, I dashed up to my room to freshen up and then puttered around, contemplating whether I should pack now or wait until the last minute.

Dathan darkened the doorway—I could sense him without looking. I swiveled to offer him a smile. "What's up?"

"You should eat."

"I'm not hungry." I slunk to the window—praying I hadn't gotten the tendency to brood from Dathan—and searched the grounds for Zack.

"You're lovesick."

Irritation welled up in me. "And?"

"So you admit you're in love with him?"

"Doesn't matter. I dumped him and he's fine with it."

"And you dumped him because…?"

I sighed. "Because even separately we'll have a difficult time surviving with the barriers we already have. And if anything happened to Zack because I was too selfish to let him go, I may as well die."

"So dramatic." Dathan clucked his tongue. "Life is too beautiful to let it pass without having exactly what you want. Especially if you have all eternity."

"Yeah?" I quirked one brow. "This from one of the biggest sourpusses I've ever met?"

"Oh, the cruelty." He clutched at his heart, then grew serious, cocking his head. "Even ancients like me can change. Having you and Zack here somehow breathed life into this dead soul."

I wouldn't read too much into that comment. Because I seriously doubted he was any less crazy than before. "You're not a dead soul. You're just… scary."

He studied me, tilting his head. "I'd hate to think I scared *you*."

I offered him a mischievous smile. "Not as much."

"Good." And then he disappeared.

What the hell was that? Whatever. I had packing to do. My parents would arrive tomorrow and I didn't want to hang around pining over Zack any longer than necessary.

As that thought formed in my head, I knew I'd be missing Zack for a hellishly long time. I couldn't imagine ever getting over him.

CHAPTER TWENTY-NINE
——— *Zack* ———

AFTER ALMOST A full twenty-four hours stewing at both my parents for keeping me in the dark, my anger toward them had eased up only a little. One day I'd completely forgive them. But not today and I wasn't going to make it easy on them.

I sat on the stone bench and sipped on my bottle of root beer, staring off at the trees swaying in the distance, the rows of colorful flowers and precisely pruned shrubs. "Let's hear all your excuses so I can get on with my day."

My mom raised one eyebrow. "I can understand why you'd be angry, but I still expect you to be respectful and listen to your father's explanation. We've earned at least that," she chastised.

No one could put me in my place like Mom. I softened my tone. "I'll listen but I can't guarantee it'll make a difference."

Renzo—also known as Lucio, also known as Dad—narrowed his eyes. "You've already decided we can't be forgiven?"

"I don't know... did I only imagine you guys treated

me like a child these past few days?"

"Zack! I raised you to give others the benefit of the doubt." My mom's eyes flared and I hung my head, knowing she was right and I wasn't being fair. "Your father and I spent some time talking and I think you may feel differently when you hear what he has to say."

I chewed the inside of my mouth to stifle the temptation to point out that whatever was about to come out of Renzo's mouth was probably a result of coaching from my mom. I sighed and leaned against the back of the bench. "I'm all ears."

"With that kind of optimism, I guess I have nothing to lose," he said wryly, his mouth tightening as he kneeled in front of me. "In all the centuries I've been alive, I've done too many things I'm not proud of. As I wrote in the letter to you years ago, sometimes I questioned even having a soul."

I remembered that letter. I'd read it every time my mom had gone into the hospital and I'd felt lost or lonely. I'd read it when the stress of going to school and working had gotten to be too much. I'd read it when I was trying to keep my mind off Autumn. And I'd read it just to remember my dad.

Crap, I was already weakening.

A slow smile crept up on his face. "And then I met your mother, and for some crazy reason she loved me."

My mom entwined her fingers with his and a pang of longing coursed through me. I'd never have that with Autumn, the knowledge that she'd be there for me day after day, her love never wavering. Autumn didn't feel that way about me anymore. My stomach twisted. I glanced away and took another pull from my root beer bottle.

Renzo rested a fist on my knee. "And then you came along. You were the one thing in my entire existence that I did right."

My brows shot up and I used the mouth of the bottle as a pointer as if I were targeting him. "And that's why you abandoned us?"

Renzo threw his head back and sighed. "I'd been mauled. Your mother believed I'd died, mourned me, and held a memorial service. Was I supposed to break werewolf law and risk her life by exposing the existence of werewolves? Not that I was in any shape to return. I was in excruciating pain with no one to help me, and unable to feed. Meds don't work well on us, by the way, because we metabolize them so quickly."

I sat the bottle on the bench and folded my arms over my chest in a gesture that must have appeared childish. What did I care what they thought? They were the ones who had to prove themselves, not me. "That doesn't explain why you didn't tell *me* you weren't dead."

"Mm-hm." His mouth slanted and irritation swept over his face. "Because six-year-old boys are so good at keeping secrets."

"I didn't stay six forever." I groaned in frustration and straightened my spine. "You had years and years to do it. What about when I turned sixteen? Seventeen? How did you convince yourself then?"

"I didn't." The worry lines between his brows smoothed

out. "We either turn humans or we cut ties with them. In order to have you in my world, I would have had to rip you out of there without your mother ever knowing who took you or what happened. I couldn't do that to either of you and I didn't think she would survive it. So I chose to give you the chance to go to a normal school without the burden of knowing that in a few years, you could be serving the werewolf king. Or on the run."

Renzo waited a beat, measuring his words. "Not contacting you was probably the most unselfish thing I've ever done and it took everything I had not to seek you out. I couldn't know you like I wanted to, yet every part of me *needed* you in my life. Instead, you shared a life with your mother, which you wouldn't have had if I'd come back. And more time with your aunt Cara and uncle Mac, your cousins."

My chest expanded and I gave in a little bit more. Bits and pieces of images flickered through my mind. I couldn't make out my dad's face, but I remembered how I felt as a little boy. I remembered how much he loved and doted on me. I'd been his whole world and he had always made sure I came first.

To cover how spineless I was rapidly becoming, I snapped up the bottle, downed the rest of the soda, and slammed the bottle on the bench. "Still no excuse for keeping the truth from me the last few months, letting me believe you were a scout, that you were a danger to Autumn."

"That was regrettable." Renzo lowered his gaze, his chin nearly touching his chest. "I've never been one of the good guys, Zack. Thinking of anyone but myself has never come easy and I haven't always made the right decisions. But I'm trying."

Well, at least he knew he was an ass. And I appreciated his effort to change that, even if he wasn't always successful. "Go on."

"Had I been less selfish, I would've been forthcoming upon seeing you at the coffee shop. But I was convinced that after all this time, you'd feel no connection to me whatsoever. I didn't want our relationship built on obligation, so I set about trying to create a real bond with you." He held his mouth straight and thin, his eyes full of sorrow and regret. "At which I failed miserably. So much for clean slates."

I wished I could change the past, but I now understood why he'd made those choices. I couldn't blame him any longer. As I stared at the man kneeling in front of me, Renzo faded away, replaced by my father. He was just a guy, desperately trying to reconnect with his son the best way he knew how.

Words bottlenecked in my swollen throat. I took a moment to steady my voice. "But... why would either of us want a clean slate when what we had was already great?"

His brows furrowed and I plowed on. "I remember when I was five, before you disappeared, and we went to the zoo. It was hot and we'd been there all day. I could barely keep my lids from drooping, but I had to see the lions. So you carried me on your shoulders, even though you'd been up all night taking the redeye and had only gotten in that morning."

"You remember all that?" His voice broke on the last two words.

"Of course. I worshipped you." Still did. I rose to stand and he did too.

He slowly inclined his head and stretched out a hand. I gathered him in a bear hug, my eyes burning and blurring.

"I'm so proud of you," he said, slapping me on the back.

When he released me, I asked, "And your reason for not telling me my mom wasn't dead?"

Renzo pinched the bridge of his nose. "Uh..."

"No." My mom patted his hand before addressing me, her eyes begging me to understand. "Telling you about me wasn't possible since he was trying to save my life the first day without the humans realizing I wasn't dead. Then you were gone. When he confided in me that he'd reconnected with you, but not in a good way, I suggested he not say anything yet. Especially given that we had no idea if I'd make it as a vampire and I could be destroyed at any moment. That allowed him more time to make things right with you."

That made sense and, in retrospect, I should never have gotten so annoyed with my mom. Anything she did, she did with conviction that it was the right thing to do. How could I stay mad at her for that? Though I wish they'd told me, none of us could change the past and undo what we'd done. I had my parents back and they weren't going anywhere. I finally had everything

I'd been wishing for.

Except Autumn. I had no clue what to do about her. The thought of her not being with me wherever I went next made me feel as hollow as the bottle I'd just emptied.

"One thing you should know..." Renzo's gaze shifted uncertainly, darting to my mom then back to me.

Crap, this was going to be bad. And he knew I wasn't going to enjoy it. I persuaded myself to stand there and take it. "Spit it out."

"I convinced Autumn that it was in your best interest to be on your own." His jaw tightened.

I wasn't sure what to think of that confession, but I didn't think my dad was trying to be a douche. He was trying to come clean and I figured I should let him. "But you changed your mind?"

"Your mother filled me in on what it was like before, that you always seemed sad. She felt guilty for burdening you with her condition but then Autumn came into your life and everything changed. You were happy with her." He hung his head. "I'm sorry I interfered."

I laughed once. "You say that because you don't know Autumn. She doesn't do anything she doesn't want to do. If she bought what you had to say, it's because a part of her already believed it. And I let her feed me that line because a part of me believes it too."

"Zack, if you truly love Autumn, talk to her." Renzo exhaled, shaking his head. "You don't want to leave it this way. Even if you only have one more day together, she should at least know how you feel about her."

"She dumped me. At this point, she probably doesn't care how I feel."

"That girl loves you, regardless of what she told you." My mom pressed a palm to my cheek. "Ask yourself this one question and forget about everything else. When you're together, do you complete each other and make each other stronger? Or are you better when you're apart? That's all that matters."

I smiled, so grateful all over again that she was here and alive. Because, yes, I believed Autumn and I made a good team. We had each other's backs and, amazingly, no matter how much time we spent together, we never grew tired of each other. I didn't want to be without her. Hell, if I had any say in it, I *wouldn't* be without her. And I was about to make a big gamble that she felt the same way. "I love you, Mom."

"I know." She patted my cheek. "Now, if I'm not mistaken, you have something you need to do."

"Before you do that," Renzo's fingers wrapped around my arm, "you should know that Autumn knew my secret for maybe a couple of hours. I asked her to give me some time, which she did."

"Fair enough." I nudged my dad in the arm with a fist. "I'll catch you guys in a little while."

He grabbed my fist, held it for a moment, then let me go. He didn't have to say it. I felt his words with that one gesture. And I was grateful to have him back too. I flashed him a smile and made my way to the palace.

CHAPTER THIRTY

—— *Autumn* ——

WITH TOO MUCH downtime, Alura had convinced King Cedric to allow her into his weapons room. She'd been in there for twenty minutes. Bored, antsy, and anxious over how Zack was getting along with his parents, I needed Alura to help take my mind off Zack and how lonely I was without him. "Alura, are you okay?" I called out.

She popped her head through the doorway. "Guns and knives, Autumn. I'm more than okay. Now leave me alone." Her eyes twinkled before she disappeared again.

Cedric sat glued to the chair at his desk and hadn't looked my way during my quick chat with Alura. Apparently he'd been swallowed by a mountain of paperwork.

I picked up the wolf-head paperweight, knocking it against the desk in the process.

He stopped squinting and peered up at me from his stack of papers. "Bored?"

I rolled my shoulders. "Just antsy."

"Problem?"

"Not sure." I rolled the paperweight between my

palms. "Been thinking about my parents. My mom's texts have been short and sometimes she takes hours to answer. She told you they'd be arriving tomorrow?"

"Yes." His gaze stayed trained on me, like he expected me to interrupt him as soon as he'd immersed himself in work again. He wasn't far off.

I bent forward, rested my elbows on his desk, and dropped my chin in my palms. "Are Ulric and his men after my parents?"

His mouth flattened to a straight line. "From the little I've gathered from your father, that appears to be the case."

The muscles in my shoulders wound up. I'd suspected as much, but was hoping my imagination had gone on a useless rampage. If my parents were indeed running from some jacked-up werewolf, they'd want to keep running.

But they couldn't avoid a fight forever, could they? Knowing they were in so much more danger, would they still insist on taking me? Could I let them leave, fully aware I may never see them again?

"I'm sorry, Autumn," Cedric said. "I'll help any way I can."

"Thank you." I buried my face in my palms and squashed the urge to cry. If I couldn't go with my parents and opted not to join SWAAST, where would I go?

The door banged open and Zack burst into the Cedric's office, his forehead creased in the center. "I need to talk to you."

Wanting to put off any conversation while he was

that intense, I picked up the wolf-head paperweight again and flipped it around. "About what?"

"You and me."

My stomach did a somersault. God, just looking at him made me want him. And I didn't want to want him. I examined the label at the bottom of the weight. "I thought we already covered that."

"Yeah, we did." He'd stopped breathing and I knew he was holding back something big. I held my breath too.

"Well…" Cedric rose and rounded his desk. Damn, I'd forgotten he was sitting there. "I need to speak to Dathan on an urgent matter. I'll be back in a few minutes."

Cedric disappeared and I stood, ready to bolt. I couldn't be alone with Zack. I was this-close to confessing how much I loved him. But what good would that do when his dad didn't want me anywhere near Zack and might not let me join SWAAST anyway? And if I were to be honest with myself about our situation, a future breakup was inevitable. Why pick up where we left off only to end it tomorrow when I leave with my parents?

And if he truly cared about me, he wouldn't have let me go so easily. "You know what? I need to finish packing."

Alura zipped out of the weapons room and halted next to us. "She finished packing last night." She wrinkled her nose at me. "Sorry." And then she zoomed out into the hallway, leaving us truly alone.

"I have plenty of other things to do." I rolled my eyes toward the ceiling. "And it doesn't include hashing out the problems of a failed relationship." I made another attempt to get past him.

"The thing is..." He sidestepped, blocking me from marching by. "You're quite good at faking it. Oscar-worthy. But no matter how hard you try, you can't make me believe that after everything we've been through, you could end it that way."

I rolled my eyes and blew my bangs off my fore-head. "Do we have to do this right now?"

"This," he wagged his finger between us, "can't be one-sided, Autumn. The last few weeks *had* to mean something to you too. It meant so much that you'd risk your life for me when Daniel wanted to make a deal. And when Charles became a threat, you offered yourself up to save me. Same with Renzo. No one does that sort of thing for someone unless they really care about them."

My mouth went dry. What could I say to Zack to get him to back off? "Maybe I did it because it was the right thing to do."

"Or maybe you did it because you care." He watched me a long moment. "I thought we were the beginning of a legend, you know? That decades or centuries from now, they'd be talking about *us* the way they do Hannah and Eli. How we defied the were-wolves, stood up for what we believed in and because of our devotion, we were willing to die as humans."

Legend... Us? He cared so much for me that he saw us together centuries from now? I might've believed that, except he'd never told me he loved me.

He chewed the inside of his mouth a moment before focusing on me again. "I'm going to put myself out there. I—"

"Zack." I hardened my voice. "It's over. Any feelings we may have had are the very thing that's going to get us killed. You're better off meeting a hot werewolf girl and falling madly in love. You can team up and fight werewolf tyranny." I gave a cynical laugh.

"There's just one problem with that." He took a step forward. I backed up and he closed the distance until the warmth from his body seeped into mine. "I don't want anyone else."

Blood thundered through my ears. I turned away, leaning a hip against the desk to steady myself. He needed to go away, because I couldn't let him back in again only to say good-bye to him tomorrow. "Well, I won't be around so you're going to have to work it out."

"Autumn." His low guttural sound burrowed through my armor. "We agreed to stay together until the end when we had no choice but to separate. We made a deal."

I threw my head back in frustration and stared at the ceiling. "In case you weren't paying attention, this *is* the end. My parents will be here soon and then I'm leaving."

He shook his head. "The end is when one of us drives away. Yes, your parents could show up and stay three minutes before taking you away. But that's tomorrow, not now."

He had me there. Except I'd still have to go through the agony of our breakup all over again. I didn't have much more fight in me, and every muscle, and every cell in my body, strained to be closer to him. "Zack, you don't want this."

"I disagree." He inched closer, but didn't touch me. My nerve endings fired to life. "With you, I'm better. I think I make you better too. And we don't know what will happen tomorrow, so why should we give up now?"

I flinched, flipping around and facing away, folding my arms over my chest. For all his insistence, he never mentioned love. Regardless, he was hurting. It was one thing to inflict pain on myself. Quite another to torture the guy I loved.

Heat emanated from his body as he came up behind me and swept his hands past my waist, splaying his hands over my belly. The sound of his quickened pulse flooded my ears. "I'm not going to give up without a fight so you may as well cave now."

The more he pushed, the more I wanted him. My powers of resistance waned and if this was our last night together, I wasn't going to waste it. I wasn't even sure anymore if being without him was actually the noble thing to do.

Or did I *want* to be wrong so I could have him? Slowly, I circled toward him and his hands slid to my hips. I covered his hands with my own, hesitating. Should I disengage or pull him closer?

As I blinked slowly, in that brief moment time stopped. My heart stuttered, skipped a beat, and my bottom lip quivered as I gazed into his deep green eyes. Zack had said he wasn't going to give up and I'd never wanted him to. I couldn't believe I'd ever considered wasting my last hours with him. "Okay."

His kiss was a blaze of pent-up fury, grief, and anxiety, and I felt it to my toes. I matched his force, my fingers diving into his hair and I propelled us against the wall. He moaned into my mouth, lifting me up so my legs could snake around his hips. Then his mouth freed mine and he buried his face in my hair.

I clung to him, soaking up his woodsy scent, the way his heart thumped and his unsteady exhale. "I don't want to be without you." After what I'd put him through, he needed to hear that.

"I know." His mouth came crashing down on mine again and he carried me to the room I'd shared with Alura.

Somehow the future didn't seem so scary and uncertain, knowing Zack cared so much for me. But after being together like this again, how the hell was I supposed to let him go tomorrow?

CHAPTER THIRTY-ONE
——— *Autumn* ———

"AUTUMN," ZACK WHISPERED the next morning.

My torso was draped across his as I dropped a kiss on his stubbly chin. His one word stirred the surface of my skin, his sweet, earthy scent bleeding into me and wending its way straight to my heart. "It's nice being like this again," I murmured. "Alura wasn't nearly as fun to cuddle with."

"That's so sad." His mouth curved up and his warm hands snaked up my spine and sent a shiver through me. "'Cause Renzo was great. We spooned all night."

I snickered, not wanting that image in my head. "You slept alone on the sofa, huh?"

He nodded and rolled us over so we faced each other on our sides. The need to kiss him consumed me and I laid my hands at the back of his head, ready to pull his mouth to mine.

My cell vibrated, throwing me out of the moment. I leaned into the bedside table for my phone and my tank top scooted up. Zack inched it up a little more and his lips trailed across my ribs, sending warmth through my middle.

I liked where this was going. As much as I wanted to see my parents, I could've used more time reconnecting with Zack. In bed. "My mom says they're a half hour away."

Zack sprung off the bed. "You can't have bed hair when your dad gets here. He'll want to kill me."

I bit my lip to keep it from twitching. "They know we're not doing anything."

"Dads worry anyway. C'mon." He grabbed the shirt he'd stripped off last night and flicked me with it. "Get in the shower."

Zack tried to swat me with his shirt again and I snatched it, yanking it and pulling him to me. I shoved him back to the bed and we tumbled. He sighed as his palm covered my cheek. "We'll work something out, okay? If we end up separating, we'll keep in touch and things will work out later."

Butterflies danced in my stomach and warmth sheathed my skin. "I hope so."

† † †

With Zack by my side, I peered out our bedroom window as a white sedan rolled up the wide, seemingly endless driveway. Had to be my parents. I dashed out into the hallway, down the several flights of stairs, and then I flew through the front door.

By the time I got to the car, my mom was getting out. She looked exactly the same. Her long, nearly black hair was a shade darker than mine, and I had to bend to hug her.

I squeezed her so tight a human would've been crushed. "Mom!"

"Sweetheart, I can't tell you how happy I am to see you." She stroked my hair then her hand froze. She leaned back to get an eyeful of me and beamed. "You cut your hair. I love it."

"Thanks." I craned my neck to get a good view of my dad, then released my mom and rounded the hood. My dad hadn't changed a bit—much taller than the average male, his hair still golden blond. And not a wrinkle in sight. I jumped into his arms. "Missed you so much."

I'd always assumed they were in their late thirties and never questioned how truly young they both looked. I hadn't seen them since learning they were shape-shifters and that I wasn't adopted. I could've smacked my forehead for not realizing ages ago there was something off about them.

Dad hefted me up off the ground and twirled us in a circle. "We won't have to miss each other for a long while. Not if we're on the road together."

Oh, crap. Which reminded me that I'd be leaving Zack. My parents expected me to drive away, not knowing when I'd see him again. Months from now? Years? Since less than an hour ago when he'd talked about our future, being without him even one day was getting harder and harder to imagine.

Or I could let my parents go. A weight lifted off my chest at the thought of keeping Zack and, just like that, my decision was made. But that meant... I slumped in my dad's arms.

It was my parents I ached for now. We'd been apart so long and we'd kept so many secrets. I felt almost desperate to bare my soul and get it all out in the open.

"Everything okay?" he asked, trying to get a glimpse of my face that was buried in his shoulder.

I threw my head back and groaned. "I'm thinking of joining SWAAST."

"What?"

I glanced over at my mom to see her eyes filled with alarm. "I want to stay with Zack. And helping his parents with the cause is the right thing to do."

My mom clamped onto my shoulders and spun me around. "The hell you are! You're a baby, barely matured into a shape-shifter."

"You can't even defend yourself," my dad growled.

My mom glared at me. "The only thing you'll accomplish is getting yourself killed."

Nothing like being ganged up on. I raised my chin. "I'm stronger than you think and I've been training for days."

"Days?" My dad's nostrils flared and I guessed he was struggling to control himself. I wasn't sure if I'd ever seen him that worked up since he was usually the calm one. "You're crazy if you think a few days of training means you're prepared for battle."

My hands shot up, palms out. "All right, all right. I agree I'm not ready to win a war yet. But I'll continue training with SWAAST." I moaned. "Mom, Dad, these guys have been oppressing our species for centuries and they'll keep doing it until someone stops them. And maybe it won't be me, but at least I can help. I can't do nothing. Isn't that how you raised me?"

"We raised you to survive," my mom said through clenched teeth. "Not take on a fight you have zero chance of winning."

"But, Mom, I can't just stand by." I glanced from one to the other, trying to get some kind of understanding from them. "You say I can't win. Maybe that's because there are too many shape-shifters who think like you. But what if every shifter out there banded together and *did* something about it? We'd have a chance then, wouldn't we? And one day there might be enough of us together to win freedom for all shape-shifters. We won't have to run anymore."

My mom and dad stood speechless. Okay, that was better than making demands of me.

"Olivia, nice to see you again." Cedric rushed to my mom and gathered her into a warm hug. I couldn't be more grateful for the distraction. When he released her, he stretched out a hand for my dad. "Quentin, been a while."

"Thanks for taking care of our girl," my dad returned, though he seemed a little stiff.

"Actually, she took care of me. She's very brave, your little one." He motioned to the front door. "Come inside and we'll catch you up."

On the other side of the door waited Renzo, Favianne, Alura, and Zack. I'd taken a few steps toward them when I twisted around and noticed my mom and dad hadn't moved. "Aren't you guys coming inside?" They exchanged glances and I said, "These werewolves aren't loyal to the king. You have nothing to worry about."

They hesitated a moment before following me inside. Cedric made introductions in the foyer, my mom wearing a constant scowl.

My mom aimed a glare at Zack. "So you're Zack."

He nodded uncertainly, his hand fluttering at his side like he was ready to shake her hand but not sure if he should offer his own. "Nice to meet you both."

She stuck close to my dad, straight faced with no sign of offering Zack a handshake. "I'm glad she had you to help her through her maturation as a shifter."

"So you're the reason my daughter is refusing to go with us?" My dad asked, his resentment apparent in his low, throaty voice.

Why were my parents being so rude? I'd have to interrogate them, but right now, I didn't want to bring attention to it. Maybe they'd chill once they saw for themselves that the werewolves posed no threat.

Zack opened his mouth, his eyes darting to me. I guess I should've given him some kind of heads up that I'd changed my mind about leaving with my parents.

"No, Mom," I cut in. "*I'm* the reason." I tugged on Zack's hand and headed toward the sitting room, giving my parents no choice but to follow. Which felt strange since nearly all our previous time in the palace had been spent in Cedric's suite or the gym.

Once we'd all taken a seat, my mom zeroed in on Renzo. "You're the leader of SWAAST?" my mom asked Renzo and once he nodded in confirmation, she went on. "My daughter informs me she's joining your group. You're in agreement with this?"

I cringed, wishing I'd given Renzo some kind of warning. He didn't like me, did he? His gaze connected with mine and I couldn't understand why he wasn't more surprised. "Absolutely."

"And you'll look after her?" my mom asked.

"As if she were my own," Renzo promised, tossing me a quick glance. I knew I owed him an explanation and even a little gratitude, but all I could do was let my mouth hang open.

"So here's the thing." Dathan stepped into the room and his presence commanded everyone's attention. "Mr. and Mrs. Rossi, you have werewolves tailing you. Extremely nasty ones. It just so happens my people have the same problem. In fact, Cedric and I suspect the guys tracking you are picking off vampires and feeding from them."

When my dad opened his mouth, Dathan held up his palm. "They're many times more powerful than they used to be and with all that power they've stolen from my people, it's only a matter of time before they catch up with you. And when they do, you won't stand a chance."

My dad's eyes grew stormy. "Ulric Vasilyev?"

Dathan hitched up a brow. "Of course. Which means your days of running are numbered."

"Who are you?" my mom asked, scooting away from Dathan which brought her closer against the back of the couch.

"I'm Dathan. I take over for Cedric when he needs a break."

A tiny gasp escaped from my mom as she slipped her hand into my dad's. "And you're telling us all this because?" my dad asked.

"I'll get there in a moment." Dathan turned to Renzo. "Once he kills Quentin and Olivia, he'll go after anyone else he and King Mortimer believe has disgraced their species. As leader of SWAAST, you'll be first on their list. Further, you're married to a vampire. And your son has fraternized with a shape-shifter."

"We know all this, Dathan." Renzo blew out an impatient breath.

My dad frowned. "We're all in big trouble, is that your point?"

"It's coming," Dathan said. "We all want Ulric and his amped up werewolves gone, but none of you can do it alone. So why don't you team up and do it together?"

My parents would never go for that. As long as I'd remembered, they hadn't made any lasting friends. They certainly wouldn't want to travel with anyone.

Obviously talking telepathically, my mom and dad eyed each other. Were they considering it?

"In view of this new information and seeing how Ulric is becoming more dangerous each day, we concede that our old ways of avoiding him might be antiquated." After a moment, my dad swiveled to face Renzo. "And that it might be mutually beneficial to team up."

"Agreed." Renzo turned to Favianne and skimmed her cheek with the back of his hand. "You understand why you can't be a part of this? Though you fared well in the recent battle, you're still frail in the sun. I can't do this kind of work if I'm worried about you the whole time. You can go with Alura and get briefed on SWAAST, get some martial arts training while you get stronger."

"I only just got you back." Favianne cupped his cheek. "But I understand what must be done. Come back to me."

"We will. I promise." Renzo kissed her softly and they broke apart when Zack cleared his throat.

We? Did he mean himself and Zack? If Zack teamed up with Renzo and my parents, I had no intention of staying behind. No way would I allow anyone to exclude me. And if I got my way, I could keep Zack while not being forced to give up my parents. Zack could get to know his dad. Everyone wins.

"Wait." My mom waved her hands in a flurry. Of course my mom wouldn't make it easy. "You're not thinking of bringing Zack into this, because I'm not taking my daughter to battle. I assumed that since Autumn is staying behind, Zack would too."

I could never ask Zack to give up the father he'd just found and no way would they leave me behind. "Zack's staying with his dad," I said. "You can't take him and not me. I'm going with you guys."

"Hell, no." My dad's face reddened. "Autumn, you're not fighting this battle."

"She's a lot stronger than you think." Dathan checked the nooks and crannies of the room, then spoke in a hushed tone. "She's had vampire blood and a healthy serving of it. I wouldn't be surprised if she were as strong as you two," he told my parents.

Both my parents adamantly swung their heads side to side. "No," they said in unison.

Silence hung in the room and I suspected everyone was waiting for me to defend myself. But my parents were right. Fighting Ulric would be dangerous and the chances of us all making it out alive were slim.

I couldn't give up though. They stood a greater chance of survival with my help and Zack's. I had to convince them of that.

"You'll never separate these two," Dathan said, saving me from myself. He jerked a thumb at Zack, then me. "And you know they're safer with you two than out on their own."

My dad's throat rumbled but Dathan drowned him out with his next words. "Rumor has it that there is a huge shape-shifter haven in Nevada. Supposedly, it's run by a shape-shifter woman who escaped from King Mortimer long ago."

My mom's eyelids flickered, giving away that she knew something about this woman. "No." She shook her head again. "Our presence will only bring her trouble. We won't risk her life that way."

"You're risking her life by *not* going to her." Dathan folded his arms over his chest. "Ulric is going to kill her and everyone else you know. Unless you stop him.

The way to accomplish that is by gathering enough soldiers. There is no other way. And now is the time, before he gets even more powerful."

My head snapped to my parents and I was about to interrogate them on this old shape-shifter when I noticed their faces. My parents had given up. Or given in.

We might all be traveling together and I would be meeting their friend from who knew how long ago. Relief swept over me and my limbs came alive with anticipation. I'd keep Zack. I'd keep my parents. For now at least.

"Go to Nevada. Get Zack and Autumn better trained for battle. And when you finally encounter these monsters, I'll be there to kill them." Dathan gave us all a smug smile.

My stomach bottomed out. Dathan was going with us? He was definitely someone you wanted on your side, but he was moody and unpredictable. Besides, between my parents and Zack and Renzo, and whoever volunteered from the shape-shifter camp, we might outnumber the werewolves chasing my parents.

"Excuse me?" my mom asked, frowning as though she couldn't have heard Dathan correctly.

"Why would you want to travel with us?" My dad asked, his head dipped to the side.

"You've noticed your pursuers are becoming gradually harder to lose?" Dathan asked. My mom and dad gave an almost imperceptible nod and he continued. "In the past, Ulric used a contact here in the palace to find vampires who were made illegally and wouldn't be missed. Kept him off our radar.

"But now, his inside source is gone and I'm afraid he's developed some kind of God complex that gives him license to kill any of us." Dathan stepped closer, as if he wanted to make sure he had our attention. "But the vampire blood isn't just making him stronger. Our blood has the same effect on him that some recreational drugs have on humans. It can be quite addicting and, consumed over long periods, can make one go insane."

"We can handle a few crazy werewolves," my mom said. "Why don't you let us deal with him?"

"Because I'm not sure you can, not by yourselves." Dathan's eyes darkened. "These werewolves who dare to hunt my kind, then take our power and leave us to die... I'll destroy every last one of them. And you two," he turned my parents, "are my bait."

That didn't sound fun. From the look on my dad's face, he agreed. "Aren't you needed here?" my dad asked. "You're the true king. Fighting werewolves isn't your job."

"Correct," Dathan agreed with a wolfish grin. "But killing werewolves is so much fun."

Renzo groaned. "Great."

"I'm not sure about this." My mom shook her head. "The more in our group, the more people to keep track of. And I don't think I like how you talk about killing werewolves. Some of those fighting alongside you, like Zack and Renzo, are werewolves. We have to be able to trust you. Without trust and honor, people die."

"You can trust that I'll do everything in my power to repay these werewolves for their courage these past few days," Dathan assured her. "And that right now I exist solely to end Ulric and anyone else who might be dangerous to Zack or Autumn."

Renzo studied Zack a long moment before turning to Dathan. "I've been waiting an eternity for an opportunity like this. I'm in."

"Good." A gleam came into Dathan's eyes. "Because my ultimate goal is to kill the werewolf king. And you all are going to help me."

"The werewolf king?" I asked, my gaze shooting to Cedric for confirmation. "Aiming a little high, aren't we?"

"Freedom to marry whomever you choose and live a life where you're not constantly running for fear that you might end up a slave. Is that goal too lofty for you, Autumn?" Cedric asked, folding his arms over his chest and scowling at my parents. "And you two. You have a daughter to keep safe. Her future is at stake now. Will you continue to run for all eternity or will you take a stand with us?"

My parents exchanged looks and energy radiated off them as they spoke silently to each other. If they bailed and rejected Dathan's idea, they'd fight harder to get me to go with them.

And if they say no, we'll still find a way to be together, Zack reminded me, slipping his hand in mind. My blood hummed at his touch and I snuck him a smile.

"We're in," my parents said in unison. The air I'd held captive in my lungs rushed out and I snapped around to face them.

Dathan sent them a triumphant grin. "Excellent. We shall leave at first light."

"We've been on the road a lot this past week. Might be nice to take a day or two." My mom gazed lovingly at me and warmth spread through me. "Spend some time with my daughter before... before everything changes."

Or before someone dies. I pushed those thoughts away. Wimping out was a great way to get myself killed or enslaved. Or I'd be forever fleeing, like my parents. No silver lining or rainbow awaited me. Maybe not ever. I'd have to roll with whatever came my way and put up the best fight I could.

"Very well. We leave two days from now."

"Wait." I raised my hand and glanced at Favianne. "We need to attend her funeral."

Favianne winced. "It's not right, my family mourning my death when I'm alive and well."

"You will remain here." Dathan scowled at her, then his gaze swept the room. "We leave in four days." He pivoted on his heel and stalked out of the sitting room.

"You can park your cars here and take the Lincoln Navigator," Cedric suggested. "It's roomy enough to fit all of you and your luggage, but with the modifications I've had done, you'll be able to move a little faster."

"Okay." My dad winked at me. "Traveling together again. Like old times."

"Yeah." So *not* like old times. For one thing, they were finally being honest with me. And this time, we were running *to* the enemy, not away from them.

"You guys can work out the details on your own. If you need anything, you know where to find me." Cedric turned to leave.

"Your Majesty," I called out and he halted. "Alura and Renzo left a little something for you in the freezer. You know, if you or any of your people are ever attacked by werewolves and need the cure."

Cedric's eyes twinkled. "Thank you." Once he and Dathan were gone, the room fell into stunned silence.

Renzo wasn't the friendliest guy I'd ever known. I couldn't help feeling that spending much more time with Dathan was a bad idea. Renzo couldn't be thinking this through. "You're okay with teaming up with Dathan?"

His head tilted side to side as though weighing his options. "He has a connection to Zack. If anything happens, he'll be able to help. And he's the most powerful vampire in existence. If anyone can survive a battle with werewolves high on vampire blood, it's Dathan. While he's hunting amped-up werewolves, he'll need the cure. That would be Zack and me."

"He's right, Autumn." Zack's thumb brushed circles over my knuckles and his eyes smoldered. *We can leave them to work out the details of the trip.*

"We'll be walking the grounds if anyone needs us." I tried to act casually as I tugged Zack toward the door and into the hallway.

You sure you want to do this? I asked as soon as we'd passed Kayla outside the door. If he had any reservations, maybe he'd tell me silently with no one else around.

Inside the stairwell, Zack shifted to fully face me and locked his fingers at the nape of my neck. *I have my parents back who I thought were both dead, a future not with the werewolf king, and an all-powerful vampire to watch over me.* He leaned in and brushed my lips with his own and I decided the stairwell was as good a place as any to make out with Zack. *And you by my side. I don't see a problem.*

Oh, we had lots of potential problems in our not-too-distant future. But as Zack said, we also had a lot to look forward to. And the best part? We didn't have to say good-bye to each other. Yet. "Then let's slay those bastards."

THE END

)

Thank you so much for reading and we hope you've enjoyed Zack and Autumn's story.
If you enjoyed this book, please recommend it to friends, reader's groups and discussion boards or tell others how much you enjoyed it by reviewing it on Amazon, GoodReads or your own site.
Thank you and happy reading!

† † †

For updates on releases, please visit www.VERONICABLADE.com.

ACKNOWLEDGEMENTS

DEAD WOLF WALKING was the most difficult to write of all my books and seemed to take forever because life challenges were constantly thrown at me. I owe all my readers a HUGE thank you for their patience. Without you guys, I might not be writing. I love you all!

I always say that it takes a village to write a book, because so many people have a hand in creating a great story. Seriously, we writers can't do it alone. I'd like to thank my mom who always cheerfully reads my first (and very rough) drafts so they are more easily read by others. Big thank you to my critiquers Pat Mason, Carol Malone, Laura Sheehan and Felice Fox. A huge round of applause to my beta readers—Courtney McGee, Emily McNew, and Danette LeBaron—for helping me iron out the rest of the flaws.

Thank you to Rose Nomura for another fabulous cover and, last but not least, thank you to my amazing and gorgeous husband who is the most neglected person in the house, yet rarely complains about his nearly non-existent wife. I'm so lucky to have you in my corner. Muaaah!

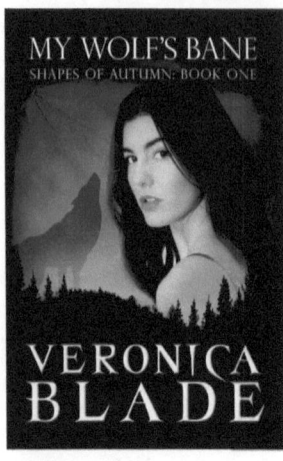
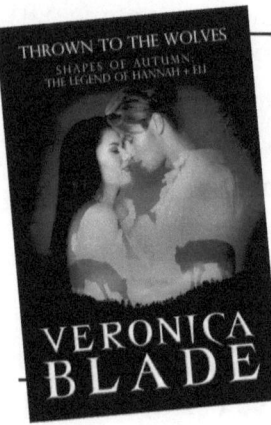

More Titles by Veronica Blade

A newbie witch enlists help from the scrumptious school bad-boy to make her life and death choice between two battling covens.

A Cinderella who spends her nights as a wolf. A prince with a taste for blood.

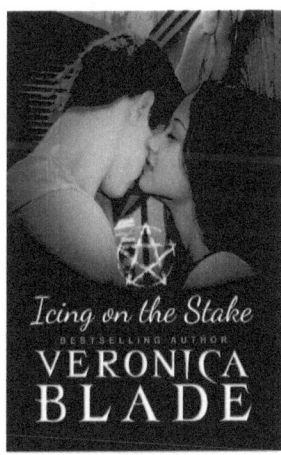

Sofia lays her hard-won anonymity on the line by saving the most popular boy in school. Worse, she's been exposed to the vampire hunters who attacked him.

The witch queen must make the impossible choice between abandoning the throne and her people, or spending eternity with the man she loves.

More Titles by Veronica Blade

Should a woman who's unable to forget her first love give "happily ever after" one more try?

When good-girl Maddie switches places with her famous bad-girl twin Jackie, she has some pretty high stilettos to fill.

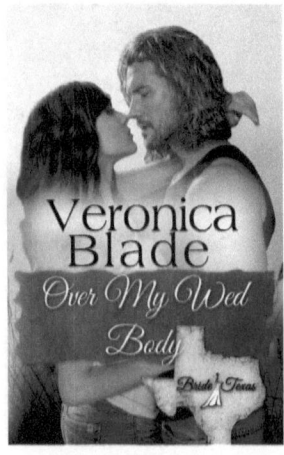

When Hunter realizes he botched the annulment of his marriage to his longtime friend, he must decide if she and their marriage are worth fighting for.

A micro trilogy including Single-Handed, Singled Out (book two) & Single-minded (book three).

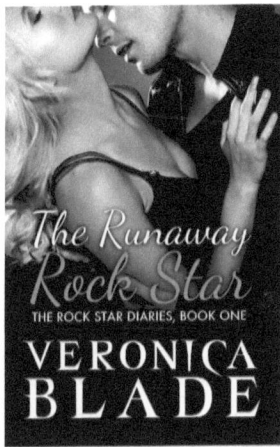
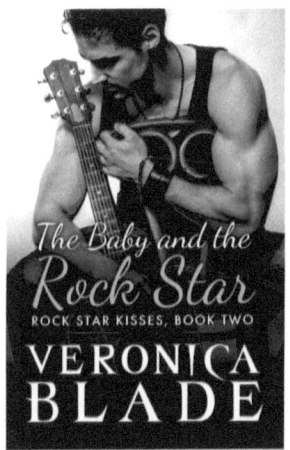

ABOUT VERONICA BLADE

VERONICA BLADE LIVES near Carson City, Nevada with her husband and furbabies but also spends a lot of time in southern California. She writes sweet romances to live vicariously through her characters. Except her heroes and heroines lead far more interesting lives—and they are always way hotter.

)

You can visit Veronica Blade on Facebook, check out her website at VeronicaBlade.com or follow her on Twitter @VeronicaBlade. You can even e-mail her at veronica@veronicablade.com. She loves hearing from readers!